SOJO

Memoirs of a
Reluctant Sled Dog

With help from

Pam Flowers

Illustrations by

Bill Farnsworth

ALASKA
NORTHWEST
BOOKS®

To Doug Pfeiffer, who always gave me a fair chance.

Text © 2016 by Pam Flowers
Illustrations © 2016 by Bill Farnsworth

Library of Congress Cataloging-in-Publication Data
Names: Flowers, Pam, author. | Farnsworth, Bill, illustrator.
Title: Sojo : memoirs of a reluctant sled dog / by Pam Flowers ; illustrated by
    Bill Farnsworth.
Description: Portland, Oregon : Alaska Northwest Books, [2016] | Summary:
    A sled dog on an Alaskan dog team relates her exciting adventures, including
    when explorer Pam Flowers and the team set out alone across the Arctic.
Identifiers: LCCN 2016006798 (print) | LCCN 2016027305 (ebook) |
    ISBN 9781943328536 (pbk.) | ISBN 9781943328543 (e-book) |
    ISBN 9781943328550 (hardbound)
Subjects: LCSH: Sled dogs—Juvenile fiction. | CYAC: Sled dogs—Fiction. |
    Dogs—Fiction.
Classification: LCC PZ10.3.F667 So 2016 (print) | LCC PZ10.3.F667 (ebook)
    | DDC [Fic]—dc23
LC record available at https://lccn.loc.gov/2016006798

Published by Alaska Northwest Books Press®
An imprint of

GRAPHIC ARTS
BOOKS®

P.O. Box 56118
Portland, Oregon 97238-6118
503-254-5591
www.graphicartsbooks.com
Editor: Michelle McCann
Designer: Vicki Knapton

Contents

PART ONE:
Mischief, Adventure, and Sled Dog School

PART TWO:
The Arctic

PART THREE:
Forever Young

Introduction

My name is Sojo (that's SO-jo, not SO-ho). For much of my life I was a sled dog on an Alaskan dog team and I had lots and lots of exciting adventures. This is my first book.

When you see a dog team in a movie or a book or maybe even in real life, you think it's just a bunch of dogs pulling a sled. But there's a lot more to it than that. There are lead dogs and swing dogs and wheel dogs and they all have important jobs. When I first saw a dog team, I didn't think I was smart enough to do any of those jobs. In fact I didn't even want to be a sled dog, but my human had other ideas. Turns out there's one more position called a team dog and they work in the middle of the team and just pull. That's where I worked. But even then I have to admit I was a reluctant sled dog.

Since team dogs don't have many responsibilities, I usually had plenty of time to look around and watch the other dogs. I always knew what they were thinking because I have a dog-given ability to silently communicate with other dogs. One day while I was hanging around the dog lot daydreaming I got this terrific idea: I should write a book about my life. I'm going to take you behind the scenes. You'll read about team meetings, petty spats, and mended friendships. You'll learn about amazing acts of courage and discover who the real heroes were on our team.

All the stories in this book are true. Well, okay, I admit I took a few liberties here and there, but mostly they're true.

—Sojo, team dog

Our Journey across the Arctic

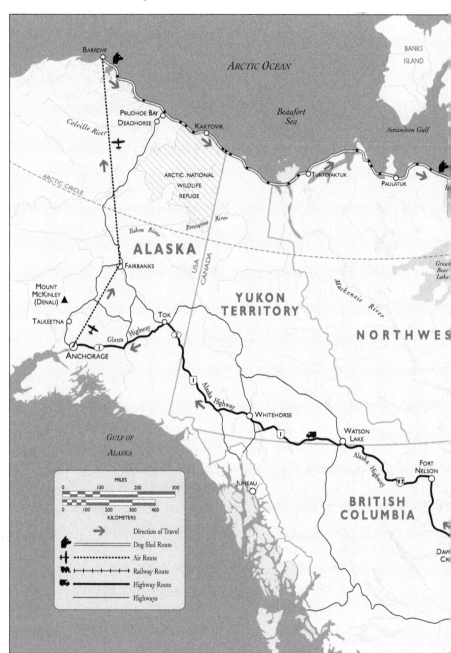

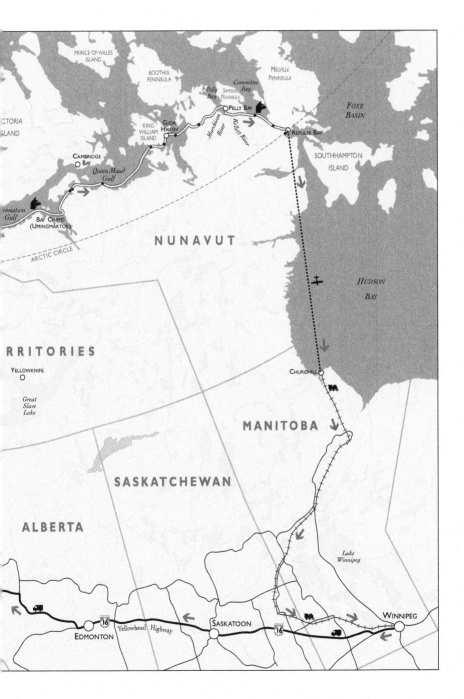

PART ONE

Mischief, Adventure, and
Sled Dog School

Chapter One

I was born in the middle of a January night during some of the worst weather anyone has ever known. It was so cold my cries of "Mew, mew, mew" froze to the tip of my tiny puppy nose. It was so windy snowflakes big enough to cover a doghouse were falling sideways!

Okay, maybe I exaggerate just a little but what do you expect? I was so young when I was born it's hard to remember exactly what the weather was like. But something totally amazing did happen that night . . . and this is no exaggeration . . . I got a human! That's right, I got a real live adult human and her job was to take care of me.

You might wonder how I could claim to know anything about my first night because puppies are born deaf and blind. Well, I could feel the cold and I could feel the wind shaking my doghouse.

When I was about two weeks old, my eyes and ears opened and I could see and hear. For the first few days my vision was kind of blurry but my hearing developed really fast. So when another human visited our kennel, I was able to hear humans speaking to one another for the first time.

"Hi, Pam," said the visitor. That's when I learned that my human had a name.

"Hi, Joyce," Pam replied. "Come see my new litter of puppies."

"How is their mother doing?" asked Joyce.

"Oh, Alice is doing fine. She feeds them and licks them with that big, wet, sloppy tongue of hers and that keeps them clean," said Pam.

"That's good. When were they born?" asked Joyce.

"They were born in the middle of the night a couple of weeks ago during that warm spell when we got a light snowfall," answered Pam.

Warm spell? Light snowfall? That's not right. What's the matter with her? I would later learn that Pam had no flair for drama and. . . .

Wait a minute! There's more than just me?

Well that explains something. Since the beginning, I've been bumping into a couple of warm, fuzzy lumps whenever I snuggled against my mom and I had no idea what they were. Now I get it! Those lumps are puppies. Turns out I have a brother! And a sister!

The humans kneeled down beside my doghouse and looked at us. Pam pointed and said, "The male hiding behind his mom is Roald. And this cute little fuzz ball with the waggly tail is Anna (AH-nah)."

When Joyce's eyes fell on me, she gasped and asked, "Oh my! Who is this little beauty?"

"That's Sojo," replied Pam.

Joyce was obviously quite intelligent and much more observant than Pam. Running her fingers along the back of my neck and down under my chin, she said beaming, "Look at her sleek, black coat and those gorgeous long legs. What a pretty white face you have, Sojo. You could be a show dog!"

I had no idea what a show dog was but that's when I first learned that I'm beautiful.

During those first few weeks, we enjoyed a quiet, happy life. Most of my time was spent playing inside our house with Anna and Roald and napping while my mom kept us warm and fed. Our doghouse faced a dense forest of spruce and birch trees and bushes sticking up through deep snow. My vision was still a little blurry but I learned to tell my sister from my brother by the way they smelled.

Obviously I had a father but I had no idea where he was or what he smelled like. Pam showed up four times a day to bring my mom a bowl of food and water and saw to it that the house was full of clean straw. While Mom was eating, Pam always showed us her teeth, which I eventually learned was something called a smile.

One afternoon when we were five weeks old, something really scary happened. We were playing inside our doghouse when Pam walked up and reached in with her bony, hairless hands. Without so much as a by-your-leave, she pulled me right out of the house and carried me off in her arms like I was a bag of dog food! I glared up at her in defiance.

How dare you handle me like this!

I had never been away from home before and had no idea what was happening. To make matters worse, we were completely surrounded by barking dogs, all lunging at the ends of their chains! They were so loud, I could hardly hear myself think! Without moving my head I rolled my eyes and counted them. Yikes! There were seven of them! I had no idea there were so many dogs in the world. I was absolutely petrified. I knew if I fell into one of those gaping mouths, it would mean instant death!

I squirmed and squirmed as hard as I could to free myself but Pam was holding me so tightly, I couldn't get away.

I began to panic! If I couldn't save myself, I was determined to save Roald and Anna.

With all this racket, I knew even if I barked as loudly as I could, they probably wouldn't hear me. I had to warn them using silent dog words and hope they were paying attention.

Roald! Anna! There are giant dogs out here trying to kill me! Quick! Run for your lives!

I don't know if Anna and Roald heard me, but somehow Pam must have been able to read my mind because she looked at all those barking dogs and bellowed, "Quiet!"

Without another woof, every dog fell silent and sat down! Pam smiled at me and said in a gentle voice, "It's okay, Sojo, I'll keep you safe." A couple of steps later she stopped and looked at me with a kind smile and said, "Sojo, there's someone I want you to meet."

She kneeled down and held me right up to the face of this huge, furry dog. He sniffed me all over with his big, cold, wet nose!

Pleeease, I beg of you! Pleeease don't kill me!

"Be gentle, Robert," said Pam in a firm voice.

Robert sat down and swished his tail across the snow.

"Sojo . . . this is your father," said Pam.

Dad? Dad, is that really you?

Yes, it's me, Sojo. I've been looking forward to meeting you, he said. Then he gave me a big, wet, sloppy kiss right across my face.

Oh, yyyuk! I blurted.

He had a sort of pleasant vinegary smell and as I looked him over, I saw that my dad was quite a handsome fellow. He had gray fur with a grayish white face, big round eyes, and an enormous bushy tail.

It was a quick visit and then I was whisked back to my doghouse. Before I could tell anyone what happened to me,

Pam picked up Anna and carted her away to visit our dad. When Pam tried to pick up my brother, Roald, he started to cry and ducked behind Mom. For some reason poor Roald was afraid of everything and every time Pam reached for him he cried louder. Finally she gave up and Roald didn't get to meet our dad that day.

The next morning Pam came and turned our doghouse around so we could sit in the doorway and look out at the other dogs. I was shocked and amazed by what happened next. Pam put a harness on our father and five other dogs and attached them to a sled with a long line. She quickly jumped on the back of the sled and bellowed, "All right, let's go!" All six dogs leaned into their harnesses and began dragging the sled down a narrow trail as though they were common beasts of burden. Pam did nothing to help them and simply stood on the sled like she was some sort of queen!

My eyes nearly bugged out of my head. I asked indignantly, *Did you see that, Anna?*

Yes, it looked exciting, replied Anna with her lips pulled back in a big doggie smile.

Exciting? Don't you think those dogs felt humiliated being forced to drag that sled?

Anna shook her head. *They were all barking and jumping up and down before they took off. It looked to me like they were having fun.*

I lay down and rested my chin on the bottom of the doorway and stared at the empty trail. Hmph! Didn't look like fun to me.

Chapter Two

When we were six weeks old Pam stuffed Anna, Roald, and me inside a box and put it on the front seat of her ancient pickup truck. The engine came to life with a loud roar and off we went. Eventually we came to a big building and Pam hauled us inside. There I met a human named Angela who was something called a veterinarian.

Angela was very smart and commented on how beautiful I was and then she stuck me with a needle! *Ouch!* "Sorry about that, Sojo, but that was your first vaccination and now you won't get sick," she said. Then she gave me a dog biscuit.

I didn't know it then but my relationship with Angela would last for my entire life.

In those days our lives were carefree and we were allowed to do pretty much as we pleased. Most mornings we played around the house. Sometimes Roald tried to steal my lunch and then he'd either go play by himself or go inside the house to nap with Mom. Anna and I spent our afternoons roaming farther and farther into the dog lot.

Pam is a very meticulous person and the dog lot was well organized. All the houses were in a big circle, so it was easy to find our way around without getting lost. Each dog had their own square-shaped house made of plywood and filled with clean straw and all the houses faced the center of the circle so everybody could see one another. Each dog was tethered to their house by a lightweight, ten-foot chain. At first it seemed cruel that they were all chained, but I would later learn that there were laws about dogs roaming loose. Keeping them home meant they wouldn't be snatched by the dog police and sent to a place called the pound where terrible things might happen.

All the dogs were quite friendly and, by the time we were eight weeks old, we had gotten to know what everybody smelled like.

Pam lived in a log cabin way over on the other side of the dog lot from us and behind her house was a tall, green cylinder. We were just two months old and had never explored very far from home, but one day we decided to investigate the cylinder. I was feeling a little nervous but Anna wanted to go and Roald decided to tag along, so right after lunch while Mom was napping, the three of us set out on an expedition. When we reached the cylinder we discovered it was giving off some very interesting odors and we became very curious.

Let's try to turn it over and see what's in there, said Anna with a sly grin.

Do you think we should? I asked hesitantly.

Anna leaped in the air and kicked the cylinder with her front feet. *Look, it wobbled! If we all jump up and kick at the same time I think we can knock it over,* said Anna, her eyes wide with excitement.

We all jumped up at the same time and kicked but the giant cylinder hardly moved. Over and over we tried but it wouldn't budge.

I know! said Anna. *Let's all jump one more time only this time let's all kick on the same side.*

We lined up side by side and Anna cried, *Jump!*

We jumped and kicked all at the same time. The cylinder rocked back and forth, back and forth. But still it wouldn't topple over.

One more time! yelled Anna.

This time we kicked as hard as we could. The cylinder wobbled and teetered on edge as though deciding what to do. We held our breath as it sloooowly leaned farther and farther to one side. Finally . . . it gave up and toppled over with a great klinky, mushy sound as it hit the ground. The lid popped off and out poured all this wonderful, delicious, smelly stuff. Slimy bits of vegetables, empty cans, gooey pieces of paper, and even some bones!

Yum, yum! Feast time! But just as my teeth were closing in on one of those bones, Pam came running around the corner of her house, waving her arms.

"Get out of there!" she yelled.

Quick, run for your lives! I yelled. We tore off across the dog lot lickety-split and jumped inside our house.

After I caught my breath, I told my mom what happened and said, *I think Pam wanted all that stuff for herself because she chased us away before we could eat any of it.*

Oh, my, said Mom, shaking her head in disapproval. *You got into the garbage. That is something no dog should ever do. Humans do not like sharing their garbage. You must promise me that you will leave all that garbage for Pam and never do that again.*

For the next couple of days we stayed close to home and kept out of trouble. Every morning Anna, Roald, and I sat in the doorway of our house and watched Pam harness the dogs and sled off down the trail. I had to admit the dogs did look excited and maybe they did enjoy it. But I was beginning to see that being a sled dog was more complicated than I first realized.

Anna, do you notice they all know how to step into their harness? I asked with my head cocked to one side.

Yes, and they're very quick about it, Anna said with a quick nod.

I cocked my head farther and said, *I think each dog has a particular place in the team and they seem to know exactly what to do. How do you suppose they know all that?*

I don't know! Then with an upward jerk of her head Anna said the most amazing thing: *But I'm going to figure it out and someday I'm going to be a lead dog.*

I stared at Anna in disbelief. *A lead dog? You can't be serious! That's the hardest, most dangerous job of all. You have to know what you're doing and you have to stay ahead of the entire team so you don't get run over. I could never do that.*

Oh, Sojo, you're such a fraidy-cat, teased Anna.

Am not.

Are too.

I felt very sad that day. I remember thinking maybe Anna was right. Maybe I was a fraidy-cat. I kept trying to think of something I could do that wasn't so hard or so scary. That's when I remembered the day Pam's friend Joyce came visiting. I remembered how she said I was beautiful enough to be a show dog.

I've got to find out what that means because that's what I'm going to be someday. I'm going to be a show dog!

Chapter Three

One bright sunny afternoon Pam walked up to our doghouse with three harnesses in her hand. She leaned forward, put her hands on her knees, and said in a chipper voice, "Guess what? You puppies are twelve weeks old and it's time to start sled dog school."

Anna wagged her tail, Roald ran inside our house and hid behind Mom, and I nearly fainted.

Pam said, "The first thing you have to learn is how to get into a harness. Which one of you is brave enough to go first?"

Anna leaped toward Pam.

No, Anna, don't go. This is puppy abuse! I shouted.

Anna paid no attention to me as Pam helped her slip into the little harness. Anna jumped up and down and ran around in circles, showing off. She made it look fun so I decided I'd give it a try.

Pam took hold of my collar and slipped the harness over my head. *Watch the ears!* She gently eased both my front legs through the loops. The harness was red and, against my black coat, I must admit I looked rather stunning. For once Roald came out of the doghouse when Pam called him, and when he got his harness on, the three of us ran all over the dog lot showing off for the big dogs and feeling quite proud of ourselves.

I ran over to my dad. *Dad! Look at me.*

You look beautiful, Sojo.

I know.

Dad shook his head and laughed.

Mom, don't I look beautiful?

Yes, dear, you look quite lovely, said my mom. *But don't chew on your harness. Pam won't like that.*

Soon it was nap time so Pam took our harnesses off and gave each of us our first taste of every sled dog's favorite treat—liver! Ummm-um.

Back in our doghouse Anna asked in a sleepy voice, *Do you still think that was puppy abuse?*

No. At first I thought Pam was going to make us pull a sled but all we had to do was try on a harness. I was worried for nothing, I said yawning.

Even I wasn't scared after awhile, said Roald.

It was a happy day and I smiled as I drifted off to sleep thinking about liver treats and dog harnesses.

The very next day Pam was in one of her rare happy moods and did something fun. "Today we start lesson number two. It's a real drag," she said with a laugh.

She put my harness on me and then took a length of string with a stick tied to it and tied the string to the end of my harness. It made a great game and I ran in circles chasing the stick until I got so dizzy I fell over.

Pam laughed and laughed. Then she helped me get up and said, "Sojo, you're never going to be a sled dog if all you do is run in circles."

It doesn't matter because I'm not going to be a sled dog. I'm going to be a show dog.

As we got bigger so did the sticks until we were dragging

around small pieces of firewood. Even though we were getting older, we still weren't chained up yet. So when we got tired of running in circles, we went back to exploring our world while dragging pieces of firewood with us.

Pam was always building something. One day we could hear her working over by the side of her house where we couldn't see what she was up to. We were going to go investigate but all that pounding and buzzing was so loud, we decided to do something else. We had never gone down the dogsled trail so we figured we would investigate to see where it led. There were lots of good smells to check out as we poked along. After awhile Roald turned around and went back home but Anna and I kept going. We came out on a really wide, flat trail that smelled weird and was covered with packed snow.

While we were standing there trying to decide what the smell was, we heard a low rumble in the distance.

Anna, what is that?

I don't know.

The rumble grew louder. I had just turned my head in the direction of the noise when all of a sudden this huge, boxy-looking monster came around a curve. It had a giant, flat nose that covered its entire face and it was heading straight for us!

It yelled at us—**BEEP! BEEP!**

Anna, quick! Run for your life!

I turned around to run but my feet got tangled in my line and I fell over.

Anna, help me! The monster's going to get me. Helllp!

Anna tugged at my line with her teeth but she couldn't untangle me. She curled her lips back and snarled at the monster as it roared toward us.

BEEP! BEEP! BEEEEP!

Anna barked fearlessly and lunged at the monster, "Woof! Woof! . . . **WOOOOF!!**"

Frightened by Anna's bared teeth, the monster swerved, just missing me as it disappeared down the trail.

Sojo, are you all right? Anna asked.

Yes, but I thought that was the end, I said trembling. *I'm glad you were here to save me.*

Just then Pam came running down our sled trail. When she saw me lying there tangled in my line, she dropped to her knees beside me. When she realized that I wasn't hurt, she scooped me up in her arms and carried me off the big trail.

"Sojo, I'm so sorry. I should have been watching you puppies better. This road is really dangerous. I'm so sorry. . . . I'm so sorry," said Pam. Tears flowed down her cheeks as she untangled my feet and then she hugged me so tightly I could hardly breathe. *It's okay, Pam. I'm not hurt.* I could see how upset Pam was and I wished she could hear my silent words the way dogs can.

We walked back to the dog lot and there sat three new doghouses lined up by our house. Roald was already tied to one house. Pam tied Anna to another and me to the last one.

We could see each other and we could touch noses, but never again would we be allowed to run loose together without Pam along to watch over us.

July and August were too hot to drag logs around so we spent a lot of time just hanging out. To stir things up, Pam started a dog-of-the-day program. On her days off Pam would come out after breakfast and turn one dog loose for the day. The first time I was dog-of-the-day I raced around the dog lot, but as soon as Pam went inside, I headed straight for the green cylinder.

Douggie, our leader and the biggest and oldest dog in the lot, called after me. *Where do you think you're going, Sojo?*

I sat down and said, *Well, umm. . . .*

In a voice loud enough for everyone to hear, Douggie said, *This is a privilege we don't want to lose. No dog-of-the-day must ever run off to the road or try to steal Pam's garbage.*

There was something about Douggie. He wasn't mean and he hardly ever barked at anyone but when he told you to do something, you did it.

Can I run around?

Yes, you can run around. Just don't run off.

And so I ran. Every time I was dog-of-the-day I would squint my eyes nearly shut and run up and down the dogsled trail as fast as I could until I couldn't run anymore. Running fast and free was the greatest joy of my life.

One of the joys of Pam's life was making things and she was spending this summer building a couple of new dogsleds.

On a pleasant, sunny afternoon while she was attaching the sled runners, our neighbor Dave stopped by. He was a dog musher too and a really big guy, maybe 6 feet 4 inches tall, and at least a couple hundred pounds.

"What you up to?" asked Dave.

"We're going on a 2,500-mile dogsled expedition. I'm going to be the first woman in recorded history to dogsled alone across the Arctic. So I'm building two new sleds for the trip."

"When you gonna do that?" asked Dave.

"We'll head up north to train in December."

"Wow!" he said. "How many of them clunker dogs you takin'?"

Clunker? Did you hear that, Anna? He just called us clunkers!

Don't worry, Sojo, Pam will stick up for us.

Pam scowled and said in an irritated voice, "Eight . . . and they're not clunkers, Dave."

I wonder which dogs are going?

"Ernie and Jocko are too old to go on such a long journey and Amy's a pet, so they're staying home." Then Pam looked over at me and said, "Everyone else goes."

Yikes! She can't possibly mean me!

"You got any sponsors for this so-called expedition?" asked Dave sarcastically.

"Not yet," replied Pam.

Dave gave a little snort and said, "Well, good luck. You're gonna need it."

Pam stood up and looked Dave straight in the eyes and said, "We don't need luck, Dave. These are good, honest, hardworking dogs and together we're going to do this."

Dave shook his head and walked away.

How can this be? I asked Anna. We're not ready. That's only four months away and we've never even pulled a sled!

Don't worry, Sojo, said Anna. *Pam will teach us everything we need to know. We can do this.*

As I watched Dave climb into his ratty old pickup truck I thought, *I just don't think I'm cut out to be a sled dog. Maybe Pam doesn't think we need luck but if I go on this trip I'm going to need all the luck I can get.*

Chapter Four

September brought cooler temperatures and with it came great changes to our lives. Pam had a big red machine called a four-wheeler that is sort of like two motorcycles hooked together side by side. Mushers use them to train dogs when there is no snow. Pam's four-wheeler was like her pickup truck, a little old and kind of worn-out, but it worked. One day she harnessed Douggie and our mother, Alice, and hooked them to the machine with long lines but there was still one harness for a third dog in the team.

"Time to start back to school, puppies," said Pam as she walked toward us.

Pam always took Anna first when we were going to learn something new, but this time she began leading me away while Anna and Roald looked on.

I don't want to go in front of that thing. What if I fall over? I'll get squashed, I protested.

Right then and there I sat down and refused to go any farther. I figured Pam was going to yell at me but instead she knelt down, cupped my face in her hands, and said softly, "Sojo, there's nothing to worry about. You are going to do just fine."

How do you know I'm worried?

Of course Pam couldn't hear my words, she just smiled with kind eyes and scratched my ears. That made me relax a little and then we walked over to the four-wheeler where she hooked me up right behind Douggie and Mom. I was now standing just a little more than a dog's length away from the front of the machine. I gulped when I turned and looked back at the front of the four-wheeler. It was so high I could barely see Pam as she climbed on.

I started jumping up and down. *Can you still see me, Pam?*

Pam turned on the machine and bellowed, "All right, let's go!" The engine roared and started slowly inching toward me.

Yikes! Please don't run over me!

When I saw Douggie and Mom lean into their harnesses, I leaned into mine and pulled with all my might and we sped up a little bit.

"Good girl, Sojo!" called Pam

As it turned out, I was worried for nothing because my first trip as a sled dog was just down to the road where I had nearly died and then we made a big, wide, sweeping turn and walked back to the dog lot. The whole time we never went faster than a slow walk. Pam took my harness off and said, "Here's your chunk of liver, Sojo. You did great and I think you're going to make a fine little sled dog."

Anna was all excited to go next and, of course, she did great.

As I watched Roald take his turn, I thought, *Maybe it isn't so hard being a sled dog. I'll have to see how things go. But 2,500 miles? I just don't know.*

By late October there was enough snow for Pam to start training us with a dogsled. It wasn't much different from pulling the four-wheeler except we sped up much faster in the beginning. At first the speed was a little scary but after awhile I got used to it. I definitely liked sled training much better than the four-wheeler because I didn't have to listen to the engine roaring behind us. What I didn't like was that Pam started hooking me up beside my brother, Roald. Don't get me wrong, Roald's okay but he gets really excited before we take off and then he barks in my ear and that hurts. Pam keeps telling him to stop but he never listens.

Sometimes we trained on roads but other times we sledded on narrow trails that wound through thick forest. I liked the trails best because it was silent except for the whisper of the sled runners gliding over the snow and the trails smelled much nicer than the road and felt softer under our paws.

One day while Pam was outside splitting firewood, Dave showed up again. He walked up the path and looked over the two sleds Pam had finished.

"Hello, Dave," Pam said. **Whack**, and a piece of firewood split in two.

"You still plannin' on traipsin' across the Arctic with them clunker dogs?" asked Dave.

"Yes, Dave, and they are not clunkers," said Pam. **Whack!**

"You find any sponsors?" asked Dave.

"No, Dave, not yet," said Pam. **Whack!**

Dave's eyebrows shot up in a look of surprise and amazement. "You told me you wrote letters to over two hundred companies and you're tellin' me none of 'em would sponsor you?"

Pam took in a deep breath and sighed. "That's right."

"Well, what'd you expect? What are ya, five foot nothin', 100 pounds soakin' wet? Why would anyone sponsor you?" asked Dave with a sneer.

Pam didn't answer; she just brought the wood-splitting maul down on another piece of firewood. **Whack!**

"So where you gonna get the money?" asked Dave.

His rudeness finally made Pam angry and she glared at him in defiance. "I'm going to borrow it, Dave. Then we're going to cross the Arctic, then we're coming home, and then I'm going to pay back every last cent," she snarled.

Dave made a little snort and shook his head, like he was going to start laughing. Then he said the most unkind thing of all: "You know, *no one* thinks you can do this. Everybody thinks you're gonna fail."

"Maybe you care what everyone else thinks, Dave, but I don't." **Whack! Whack!**

"Well, good luck because that's the only thing that's gonna get you across the Arctic," said Dave.

Pam straightened up and watched Dave as he walked back down the trail to his ratty old truck. With the wood-splitting maul clenched in both hands, she muttered something under her breath that I couldn't hear and then turned back to the woodpile.

Whack! Whack! Whack!

Chapter Five

By November we dogs were becoming a real team and, much to my surprise, it felt good to be a part of it. In fact, I had actually come to enjoy our daily training runs. Even Pam seemed happy and I assumed she had forgotten all about her starry-eyed plan to dogsled across the Arctic.

As I look back on those days, I realize all the signs were there but somehow I missed them. Pam hooked us up in bigger and bigger teams until all eight of us were working together in one team. We trained longer, traveled more miles, and hauled more weight on the sled each day. Pam bought bags and bags of dog food and, in her meticulous way, put each one in a heavy plastic bag, then into a burlap bag, and then tied and taped the burlap bag shut. For reasons I didn't understand at the time, she loaded them into her truck and hauled them away. Even when Pam quit her job I just figured she wanted to spend more time with us.

Then, on December 2, everything changed. Pam rented a huge truck, put each of us in an airline kennel inside the back of the truck, stuffed the sleds and a bunch of gear in, and drove off down the highway. Three hours later we arrived at a place that was very noisy and confusing. It would have been so much nicer if Pam had told us what was happening, but I could see she was very nervous and when she gets nervous she doesn't say much to anyone.

Where are we, Mom? What are those big trucks with wings? I asked.

We are at the airport, dear, and the big trucks with wings are called airplanes, answered Mom.

Why do they need wings? I asked.

So they can take off and fly, said Mom.

Fly??? Up in the air like the birds? I asked.

The big dogs and I have all been in them and it's quite safe, said Mom.

Before I could ask any more questions, a short, heavy machine rumbled up. It used its long, powerful arms to load our kennels into one giant kennel and then the giant kennel was loaded into the belly of the airplane. I couldn't see outside but after awhile I could feel the airplane moving as it roared down what seemed to be a very long road. Everything around us was rattling and shaking and then, like magic, the ride smoothed out, so with nothing else to do, I went to sleep.

Several hours later I was awakened with a start as the airplane bumped down and sped noisily along another long road and then stopped. The door to the airplane opened and another short machine rumbled up and lowered us to the road with a thump. I looked out of my kennel and felt a blast of freezing cold air.

Mom, where are we?

We're at an airport in the Arctic, said Mom.

I stared at Mom in disbelief. Slowly my heart sank as I finally understood what was happening. We really were going on a 2,500-mile dogsledding expedition across the Arctic. This was my worst nightmare coming true. I knew I could help train the other dogs and even help drag a heavy sled

around for hours, but I was absolutely certain that I could never make it across the Arctic.

As Pam pushed a sled past me I called out, *Pam, you're making a terrible mistake!*

Pam, please, please . . . don't make me do this!

Of course she couldn't hear my silent dog words.

Trapped in my kennel at an airport in the Arctic, I felt helpless and scared. But there was nothing I could do and so I sat silently waiting for whatever was going to happen next.

PART TWO

The Arctic

Chapter Six

I was watching the airport beacon flashing white then green then white then green over and over when a couple of Pam's friends showed up in two pickup trucks.

One man jumped out and shook hands with Pam. "Welcome to Dead Horse," he said.

Dead Horse? I don't see any dead horses. Come to think of it, I don't even know what a horse is. Does anybody know what a horse is?" I asked.

Everyone was busy watching the humans so nobody answered me. Pam and the men quickly loaded everything into the trucks, including us dogs. Standing between the two trucks Pam pointed to our kennels that were being put back on the plane and said, "Say good-bye to your kennels, puppy dogs. We can't take them with us on an expedition so you're all going to have to get used to sleeping without them."

No sooner had we settled in for the ride when we arrived at a parking lot beside a collection of huge, gray, metal buildings. The airport was no longer in sight but the whole place was lit up with big lights on top of tall poles and I could see a bunch of giant trucks nearly buried in snowdrifts beside the parking lot. Pam strung a very long chain called a picket line between two of the trucks. Spaced along the picket line were shorter chains and Pam tied us to those.

Our first night was dreadful. We snuggled down behind the snowdrifts and trucks as best we could but we could still feel the freezing wind. It was very late, so right after Pam set up her little red and white tent, she went in search of food for our dinner. Apparently she expected all those bags of dog food that she had so carefully bagged and shipped to be here waiting for us but she couldn't find them. The longer she looked the more upset she got.

Finally, her voice filled with frustration, Pam told us, "Look, it's almost midnight and I know we're all tired and hungry but there's nothing I can do about that now. I promise, in the morning I will find our food and then we will all eat."

Pam looked exhausted as she climbed into her tent. I wanted to tell her that we were okay, that dogs, like wolves, can occasionally go two or three days without eating if they have to. Instead I tucked my nose under my tail and went to sleep.

Before first light the next morning I opened my blurry eyes just in time to see Pam walk up with one of the missing bags of dog food on her shoulder.

Pam plunked the bag down and said with a big smile, "Turns out people in Dead Horse go to work early so while you dogs were still snoozing I found someone who showed me where our food was stored."

Pointing across the parking lot, she said, "All this time it was right over there in that building. The guys here had locked it up to keep it safe, so that's why I couldn't find it last night."

We sat like little statues staring at the bag of food and drooling while Pam went into another building and came back with a bucket of warm water. She dumped half the food into the water and when it was soft and warm, she put a bowl down in front of each of us that was filled to the brim with yummy food. That was the best breakfast I'd had in a long time.

We dogs spent the rest of the day watching Pam haul gear and supplies over to our camp and sort everything into five neat piles; our food, her food, fuel, our gear, her gear. At the end of her long and busy day, Pam was happy but worn-out, so after feeding us dinner, she crawled into her tent and went to sleep.

The incident began sometime later. I was snuggled in and fast asleep when I woke up to the sound of something shredding. I looked to see what was happening and there, under the glare of the tall lights for everyone to see, was my grandmother, Lucy, ripping open a burlap bag. Somehow she had slipped her collar and, using that incredible dog nose of hers, she had managed to find where the food bags were stacked. I knew it was one of Pam's food bags because there was a steak poking out through a small hole.

I could hardly believe it—my grandmother was a thief!

By now everyone was awake and every eye was on Lucy as she dragged the heavy bag past us. I guess she was going back to her spot on the picket line where she thought she could keep all the steaks for herself.

Douggie was closest to the bag, so as Lucy dragged it past him, he leaped at the bag and grabbed it with his teeth. He gave a hard tug and a steak fell out through the hole and he snatched it up.

Lucy continued dragging the torn bag past us. More steaks fell out through the hole and tumbled across the snow. Suddenly everyone was lunging for the bag with their necks stretched and jaws snapping.

Lucy, give me that bag! said Robert.

No, give it here! called Matt.

Save me a steak! yelled Roald.

When it was over, every one of us had somehow managed to snag at least one steak.

The next morning Pam crawled of her tent and stretched her arms to the sky. Her good morning smile slid off her face when she saw the shredded bag. She picked up the bag, clenched it in her fist, and glared at it in disbelief. Shaking it in the air, she demanded, "Who did this!?"

As her eyes swept over our faces looking for the guilty dog, Pam finally noticed that the picket line consisted of seven dogs and a collar. Lucy was standing on top of a snowbank next to one of the trucks.

"Lucy!" Pam said in disbelief. "It was *you*? I can't believe you would do such a thing."

Like all dogs everywhere, my grandmother was a skilled actor and knew exactly how to make it appear as though she felt guilty for doing something wrong. Lucy flattened her ears against her head, let her tail droop, and stared down at the snowbank. She was the very picture of guilt and shame. However, as a dog, I can tell you Grandma felt no remorse whatsoever for having stolen Pam's food and, given the chance, she would do it all over again.

"Lucy, you should be ashamed of yourself, you're nothing but a lowlife thief! I've half a mind to let you go hungry for the rest of the week," Pam yelled in a threatening voice.

I wanted to remind Pam that dogs, like wolves, can go two or three days without eating. Instead I tucked my nose under my tail and tried to go back to sleep.

After putting Lucy's collar back on and tying her up, Pam moved all of the food bags far away from us dogs. Of course she never carried out her threat against Lucy.

The next day she took us out in two four-dog teams on our first training run in the Arctic. Uncle Matt and my mom, Alice, ran in lead while Anna and I ran behind them. As we rounded the last big truck, I couldn't believe my eyes. Ahead of us was a vast, gently rolling plain covered in snow that stretched as far as I could see. I remembered that Pam had once told us about a place called the tundra and this had to be it.

Anna, look at this place. It's huge. There's not a tree in sight and there are no trails. Hey, how will we know where we're going? How are we going to get back if there's no trail to follow? I asked.

Don't worry, Sojo. Uncle Matt and Mom have been in the Arctic before and they know what they're doing, said Anna.

Sure enough, after awhile, Pam bellowed, "Matt, Alice,

gee!" and they turned right. Then she called "gee" again and they turned right again and swung over onto our outward-bound trail and followed it back to our camp.

They make everything look so easy but being a sled dog still seems so complicated, I said.

Anna pulled her lips back in a big doggy smile and said, *I'm watching everything they do and one day I'll be lead dog on this team.*

Back in the parking lot, while Pam was taking off our harnesses, a man named Bill came out of one of the buildings. Bill was the supervisor of the company that owned the big trucks and was kind enough to let us camp next to the parking lot. He would be a big help to us while we stayed in Dead Horse.

He walked over to us and asked, "How's training coming?"

"Fine," said Pam with a smile. "For now I'm only going to make short runs to give the dogs a little exercise. It's a lot warmer down in South Central Alaska where we live so their coats are too thin for the Arctic. For now I want them to use their energy to grow thicker coats so they can handle the cold better."

He nodded and said, "Good idea. They sure do look happy and healthy." He stood there for a few minutes, shivering in the cold, and then he pointed at me and said, "But that one, she's beautiful." I knew right then that Bill was a very smart guy.

It stayed cold and mostly we just hung out growing our coats thicker. Because there were so many trucks driving everywhere, it was too dangerous for any of us to run loose, so we couldn't have a dog-of-the-day program. But as long as the weather was good, Pam did take us out in four-dog teams every day for short training runs and that was always fun.

Chapter Seven

Once we had been living in Dead Horse for about two weeks Pam decided we were ready for something more adventurous. She put us all together in one big team of eight dogs. Douggie and Robert ran in lead, Anna and Mom ran behind them in swing, next Roald and I ran together, and Lucy and Matt ran in wheel. It was just like back home. As soon as Pam stepped on the sled, Roald barked right into my ear.

Stop that! I said.

Woof! Woof! Roald barked again.

Before I could complain anymore we took off. For some reason we were pulling two sleds and that made the going slow because they were really heavy.

After awhile, Pam bellowed, "Whoa! That's it for today."

We had never traveled so far from Dead Horse before and I had no idea what was happening. *Where are we? How far did we run? Are we still in the Arctic?*

Yes, dear, we are still in the Arctic, answered Mom.

Why are we stopping in the middle of nowhere? I asked.

It's December, Mom explained, *the darkest month of the year. There's no sun in the Arctic now and daylight only lasts about three hours. We are stopping so Pam can make camp before it gets dark and then we'll sleep here tonight.*

Since it was the middle of the afternoon, we all lay down for a nap, the way we did every day. Later, after feeding us dinner, Pam went inside her tent and the older dogs went to sleep. But this was our first night to sleep out on the trail and Anna, Roald, and I were way too excited to sleep, so we decided to stay up late and play tug-of-war with the gangline. In no time we had it completely shredded into one big, stringy mess. Since we didn't have anything else to play with, we finally settled down and went to sleep.

The next morning I awoke to discover that during the night my legs had gotten tangled in shredded gangline. When Pam crawled out of her tent to feed us breakfast, I jumped up and fell over right at her feet. All I could do was lie there in a big heap and hope that somehow she wouldn't notice me.

Of course the first thing she did was notice me. Her face scrunched into a deep frown and she shook her head in disgust. "What have you done to the gangline?!" she demanded.

It wasn't just me! I protested.

Pam knelt down to untangle my legs and that's when she noticed that Anna and Roald were also tangled in mangled gangline. *Yikes! We're gonna get it now.*

It took awhile to untangle so many legs and feet, which gave her plenty of time to give us a good tongue-lashing. "I thought you puppies were more grown up than this. Didn't your mother teach you not to chew on lines and harnesses? The three of you are an embarrassment to your team. You're bad! Bad, bad, bad!"

As she walked off in a huff, Pam glanced over her shoulder and said, "Since you've been chewing on the gangline all night, maybe you don't need any breakfast."

Of course we did get breakfast but Pam fed us last.

We didn't know it then but the next two days were going to give us puppies a chance to prove that we were actually growing up—well, a little anyway—and that we were becoming tough sled dogs.

Pam had to change the gangline so we got off to a late start and then we made another run about as long as the day before. When we stopped for the day, Pam stepped off the sled and looked over across the tundra. Instead of unharnessing us, she started digging around in her sled bag and finally hauled out a long, narrow, pointed thing called a snow saw. She used it to cut a bunch of snow blocks and then used the blocks to build a long, curved wall slightly taller than us dogs. By the time she was finished the wind was blowing hard and snow was drifting across the tundra.

She quickly took our harnesses off and picketed everyone behind the wall out of the wind. Pam looked at us puppies and wiggled her eyebrows up and down. "Oh, oh. Looks like you puppies are going to experience your first really serious Arctic blizzard. Whatever you do, don't knock that wall down . . . unless you want to blow away," she said with a sly smile.

Blizzard?! Blow away?! Mom, are we going to blow away? I asked.

Just do what you are told, dear, and everything will be fine, replied Mom.

After dinner Pam did something very strange. She soaked more dog food in warm water and then, for some reason, dumped it all out on the snow behind her tent where we couldn't get to it. She squashed it flat with the bucket lid and then climbed back into her tent without giving us any of that food.

What did Pam do that for? We could have eaten that, I said.

You'll find out tomorrow, Sojo. Now go to sleep, said Mom.

I wasn't really sleepy so I stuck my head up above the snow wall to look at the blizzard. Blam! A blast of freezing air struck me right in the face. In a heartbeat snow plastered my eyes shut and shot down my throat, nearly strangling me. *Yikes!* I jerked my head down and wedged myself in between Anna and Roald. As the night wore on the wind grew stronger and stronger. It roared through camp making so much noise I couldn't sleep. Snow blew sideways across the top of the wall and some of it fell down, slowly burying us.

Sometime in the night I must have finally dozed off because the next thing I knew everyone was standing up and shaking the snow off, and Pam was standing in front of us explaining that it was too windy to go anywhere.

Thank goodness, I said sleepily to Anna. *If we go out in that storm, we'll blow away never to be seen again.* Since I was still tired from so little sleep, I ate breakfast and went right back to sleep.

Around midday I woke up to the sound of metal striking something solid. All that dog food Pam had poured out behind her tent had frozen into a big, round slab and the noise came from Pam chopping it up into pieces with her hatchet.

"Care for a little dog-food pizza?" asked Pam as she walked along tossing pieces onto the snow in front of us.

Pizza? What's pizza? I asked.

Eat it, dear. It's good for you, said Mom.

But it's frozen! I'm not going to eat this stuff.

Mom explained, *Sojo, there's nothing in there but dog food and frozen water. Pizza is what Pam always feeds us for lunch when we are on trips. The dog food gives you energy and the ice will melt and get some water into you.*

I looked at Anna and Roald. They were both standing there staring down at their pizza as though they thought it was going to bite them.

How are we supposed to eat this stuff? I asked.

Then Anna looked around at the big dogs and said, *They're all just munching it right down. Maybe we should try a little bit and see how it tastes.*

Okay, you go first, I said.

Anna bit off a little chunk and chewed it up.

It's not bad, said Anna.

I bit off a tiny piece. It didn't taste all that bad but what I really liked was the crunching sound it made when I chewed it. That was fun so the three of us dived in.

Crunch, crunch, crunch. Crunch, crunch, crunch. Crunch, crunch, crunch, crunch, crunch.

Late the next day the storm finally broke and we took off. Four days later we arrived at a place called Bullen. The last part of that day was amazing because Douggie led us for a really long time in total darkness and yet he somehow managed to get us exactly where Pam wanted to go. Of course I suppose Pam had something to do with helping us stay on course, but she wore glasses and they stayed fogged up from the cold, so she couldn't really see much. I think most of the time she had no idea where we were going and it was really Douggie who did most of the navigating.

Apparently Pam really liked Bullen because when we pulled in she jumped off the sled and went wild. "Yahooo! Thirty-eight miles across the tundra without a trail. That's an achievement to be proud of and tonight we celebrate!" she shouted.

Pam took our harnesses off and turned us all loose. Suddenly no one felt tired anymore and we took off to explore. Since Bullen was nothing but a small cluster of gray, flat-roofed, one-story, abandoned buildings there wasn't much to investigate but it was still fun sniffing and running around anywhere we wanted to go. Every door to every building had long since been blown open so we were able to get inside the buildings but they were mostly empty except for big snowdrifts.

After Pam had set up camp and fixed our dinner, she called, "All dogs come!"

Pam had a picket line set up for us behind one of the buildings so we would be out of the wind. After she clipped us in, she gave each of us a huge dinner and then we all went to sleep, tired and happy.

The next day was too stormy to travel so we dogs played and took long naps. For us it was a relaxing day but Pam had work to do.

Mom, Pam took some bags of dog food off the sled and put them over in that building. Now she's taking some of her food and some fuel over there. Are we moving to Bullen? I asked.

No, dear. She's just putting in a cache, replied Mom.

What's a cache? I asked.

It's a bunch of supplies left somewhere to be picked up later. When we go past here on our trip across the Arctic, these supplies will be here so we don't have to haul everything we need on the sleds at one time and that will make the sleds lighter, explained Mom.

Sure enough, I watched as she put two cans of fuel and half a bag of her food inside a small building. She closed the door nearly shut, leaving a crack too narrow for animals to get in but wide enough so it couldn't freeze shut.

The next day when we headed back to Dead Horse, our sleds were a lot lighter and we made good time. Pam gave us an extra big dinner and we started to settle down for the night, happy to be back at our old campsite. But before Pam headed off to have dinner with her friends, she spoke to us:

"That was our first long training run and I'm proud of you dogs. It's Christmas Eve and I have a special gift for each of you," she said with a big smile.

She reached into her food bag and pulled out eight steaks! Wow! Eyes popped and mouths drooled.

Can you believe this? exclaimed Douggie as he gently accepted his steak.

Wow! And I didn't even have to steal them, said Lucy.

Everyone laughed. We gobbled down our steaks and scoured the snow for every last morsel. Finally, we settled down for a blissful night under a starry sky, our bellies full of steak and our heads filled with dreams of running free in a place called Bullen.

Chapter Eight

For the next month we sledded back and forth across the north coast of Alaska laying in caches, getting stronger, and gaining experience in traveling through a land with no trees or trails.

During those training runs we worked hard every day. We learned a lot of things, like how to stay safe in a blizzard, how to travel over long stretches with absolutely no trail, how to travel in the dark without getting lost, never, never to chew any lines, and we learned that sometimes Pam likes to tease us. But best of all, we had learned to love dog-food pizza.

The first thing Pam did every day when she climbed out of her tent was announce the date and temperature. That's how I know that on January 19 the temperature was -43°F. The wind was so strong that snow was blowing sideways. Cold and windy? Hmm . . . Somewhere in the back of my mind it all seemed so familiar. Oh yeah, now I remember. It was just like the night I was born.

Pam remembered too and she declared, "You puppies are one year old today and we're going to celebrate!" She hauled out a bag and held it up in front of her. "You know what's in here? Hamburger patties! I brought them along just for today and there's enough for everyone to get three patties!!"

Everyone barked and jumped up and down with excitement. While we stuffed ourselves with burgers Pam serenaded us by howling a little happy birthday song. When a human howls it's called singing and it sounds very weird. I must say that I prefer dog howling but I did appreciate her effort.

January 24 was another big day. In fact, it was *the* big day. Bill showed up and loaded most of our sleds, gear, and food into a big truck. Two more of Pam's friends loaded us dogs and the rest of our stuff onto the backs of two smaller trucks and we left our camp by the parking lot. The three trucks drove together about forty miles along a road that crossed the huge Prudhoe Bay oilfields. When we arrived at the edge of the tundra and everything was unloaded, Pam thanked the three men for helping us and then they turned around and drove away. Once again we were alone.

Wow! This was it! We were about to officially begin our big journey. Pam checked her thermometer and announced it was -34°F. The sky was clear blue and a gentle breeze drifted across the tundra toward us. I could tell Pam was excited because she was moving around quickly, checking every strap and tie-down on the sleds and she was softly howling.

As we stood there in our harnesses and thick, warm, fur coats and our tails wagging overtime, I must admit I felt a little twinge of pride to be on the team. We had all worked hard to get fit and strong and Pam had gotten us used to the discipline of a daily traveling routine: warm breakfast, pull sleds, pizza for lunch, nap, pull sleds, camp, warm dinner, and plenty of sleep. Simply put, we were a team and we were ready.

At 1:30 in the afternoon, Pam climbed on the sled and bellowed, "All right, let's go!"

The wind was in my face and I felt a little cold and I

wished we could wait until it warmed up more, but by now I had learned to accept many things even though I didn't really like them. So, with a deep sigh, I leaned into my harness and pulled.

Thankfully, we didn't travel very long before Pam stopped and set up camp. After we finished eating Pam sat down beside lead-dog Douggie and showed him a big, flat, floppy thing called a map.

"We're here just outside of Dead Horse," said Pam, pointing to the map. "We want to travel across the Arctic from Barrow to the east side of Canada, but Barrow is way over here, 220 miles west of us. So to get to our official starting point, we have to travel 220 miles in the wrong direction. Once we get to Barrow, we'll turn around and start our trip east."

One thing dogs are good at is hanging around listening to people talk and acting like they are interested. Whenever Douggie poked his nose into the map where Pam pointed, we all knew he had no idea what she was talking about any more than the rest of us did. But at least he gave Pam somebody to talk to.

What I remember most about the first few days of our trip was how cold it was! On the fifth day out of Dead Horse Pam told us, "The temperature has dropped to -45°F."

Yikes, I didn't know it could get that cold, I said.

Pam continued, "This cold is going to make the snow change. It'll be a lot coarser and that will make pulling the sleds harder. One good thing, though, is that the wind has shifted and it's coming from behind us now, so that will help push us along."

Between the deep cold and hard pulling, we were getting pretty worn out but everyone still pulled hard.

Thank goodness for storms. In just a few hours the temperature rose to a balmy -24°F, the wind picked up, and for the next three days we were stuck in camp while a storm raged. Ahh, there's nothing like snuggling in amongst your teammates behind a snow wall, snoozing away the hours, and being served warm meals by your human every few hours. I was beginning to think that maybe being a sled dog wasn't so bad after all.

When the storm blew itself someplace else, we took off

again. I felt a bit stiff from lying around for so long, but of course Anna was raring to go. A few days later I was shocked and amazed when Pam moved Anna up beside lead-dog Douggie so she could start learning commands. Poor Douggie. I could see it made a lot of extra work for him because every time Pam bellowed "gee" Douggie had to shove Anna to the right and every time Pam bellowed "haw" he had to drag her to the left.

I guess she did okay for a beginner because after that, for part of each day, Pam put Anna up beside Douggie for more lead-dog training. Anna was thrilled and she became happier and happier as the days passed. I must say I got a little tired of her eager-beaverness.

One day we were sledding along pretty slowly when I yelled, *Caribou!*

You're smelling things again, said Roald.

No, I'm not. Look, there they are, dead ahead, I said.

Everyone looked ahead and, sure enough, there were hundreds of caribou grazing on the tundra. Suddenly, the chase was on! We took off after those caribou so fast we nearly melted the snow. Pam hung on to the bouncing sled for dear life and, since the caribou were heading toward Barrow, she let us run. When we finally ran out of breath, we gave up and stood panting as the caribou disappeared over the horizon.

Yee doggie! That was fun! I shouted.

On February 9 another storm was slowly overtaking us and, around the middle of the day, Pam called a halt. I thought she would set up camp but instead she just had us all hunker down behind the sleds for a rest. After about an hour she roused us up and told us to get going. I tried to tell her, *Pam, you're making a mistake. We shouldn't travel in a storm,* but of course she couldn't hear me. I wasn't very happy but I leaned into my harness and went to work anyway.

After a couple of hours the storm started letting up and then I saw the most wonderful sight. Out of the darkness appeared a dim flash of green, then white, then green, over and over. They were the same colors that flashed at the Dead Horse airport.

Look, everybody! I shouted. *Look at those flashing lights! Maybe we're going to fly back home.*

Everyone got excited and we leaned into our harnesses and pulled as fast as we could. But it turned out the lights weren't nearly as close as we thought and after a long time they still looked very far away. Sometime in the middle of the night we finally pulled into the outskirts of Barrow and flopped down, exhausted.

Pam said we had traveled forty-two miles. No wonder it took so long to get here. That was our longest day so far.

The next day Pam found her friend Craig's house and we camped in his backyard. Of course we didn't fly home but for five luxurious days we lounged around doing nothing but eating and napping in the sunshine. Pam stayed at Craig's house, which was good because she was sick with a nasty cold.

One afternoon while the other dogs were napping, Mom said, *You worked really hard coming over here, Sojo. You never quit even when things got hard and I want you to know I'm really proud of you.*

Hearing my mom tell me she was proud of me made me feel happy inside. *Yeah, it was hard sometimes but it wasn't as bad as I thought it was going to be.*

Do you still want to be a show dog, Sojo?

Maybe, I'm not sure. I know I like going different places with the team and learning new things.

That's good, Sojo. I'm glad, said Mom with a little smile.

Chapter Nine

On February 14 Pam woke us up from our nap and announced, "They said on the radio there was a storm coming but look how warm and sunny it is. There's not a cloud in the sky and it's only five below zero. I do believe it's a perfect day for dogsledding, so we're leaving."

It was early afternoon before Pam got the sleds loaded. There was no crowd of cheering fans; it was just Pam and us dogs. We were camped in the middle of a neighborhood and, I realized as Pam was putting my harness on me, I couldn't even see the tundra.

Craig and another guy showed up and everyone stood around talking. Then Craig walked back to the trailer sled and sat down while his friend sat on the front sled. Pam walked around the sleds one last time, carefully checking every last detail. Satisfied everything was ready to go, she said, "Thanks for riding over to the tundra with us, you guys. If anything goes wrong it will be good to have a couple of seasoned dog mushers around to help out."

Pam pulled the snowhook out of the snow and nervously squeaked, "All right! Let's go!"

What I witnessed over the next few minutes explains

why we all admire and respect Douggie so much. Without so much as a woof, Douggie set off with confidence. He led us across Craig's backyard, past a snowmobile, between two houses, around a neighbor's garage, down a driveway, across a road, across a field, around a telephone pole, and out onto the tundra. He never stopped or got lost even once.

What a lead dog! There's nothing Douggie can't do, I said proudly.

Pam stopped us briefly so Craig and his friend could jump off the sleds. They shook hands with Pam and everyone waved good-bye.

"Good luck!" called Craig.

It was a beautiful blue-sky day as we set off across the gently rolling tundra. We were finally heading east on our 2,500-mile journey and we couldn't have asked for a more perfect beginning.

After that it was silent except for the whisper of the sled runners over the snow. Everyone soon relaxed and enjoyed being on the go again as we dropped into our familiar, steady pace.

One day sledding conditions were particularly difficult because it was very foggy and hilly. It would be easy to get lost out here and Pam needed a lead dog with more experience than Anna, so she put my dad, Robert, up front with Douggie. After we had been traveling for a couple of hours I said to Anna, *This fog makes everything so white it's impossible to tell where the land ends and the sky begins. How does Douggie know where to go?*

I don't know, said Anna, *but I'm watching everything he does and I'm going to figure it out.*

As usual, Anna was sure she could learn to do anything. But to me the job of a lead dog was so difficult and complicated that I knew I could never figure it out.

As the day wore on the fog became even thicker and the land was an endless series of rolling hills. Normally this wouldn't be such a serious problem but we were getting very low on supplies and we needed to find our next cache. Pam was sure the fog was throwing Douggie off course and that he was going too far south. If we didn't get back on course we were going to miss our cache.

"Haw," bellowed Pam as she tried to get Douggie to move more to the north.

Douggie swung to the left and then immediately swung back to the right.

"Haw!" Pam shouted.

Again Douggie swung left and then back to the right.

Pam was getting angry and yelled, "Douglas, haw! Haw!"

Time after time Douggie refused to stay left. Pam was now furious. Just as she yelled some words that I couldn't understand, we crested a high hill and there in the distance was a piece of driftwood sticking up out of the snow and beside the driftwood sat our cache! The moment we saw it we surged ahead, running as fast as we could. Seconds later we pulled up beside our pile of arctic treasure and stopped. Pam got off her sled and walked up to Douggie. We expected she was going to give him a good tongue-lashing, but she didn't. Instead she looked down at Douggie and a big, warm smile spread over her face.

She shook her head in amazement and said, "Douggie, I don't know how you do it but you know better than I do where we're going. I'm sorry I yelled at you."

Douggie never held a grudge. When Pam kneeled to give him a big hug, he woofed and slurped his tongue across her face in a big, wet, sloppy kiss that knocked her right over. Anna thought that was very funny and started barking and bouncing around. Soon everyone was barking and bouncing.

Group howl! I shouted.

Everyone threw their heads back and howled to the sky. Pam laughed and threw her head back and joined right in. We were a team again and everyone was happy.

We took a nap while Pam sorted through the cache and loaded everything onto the sleds. As we took off, I have to admit I felt a little better knowing that even Pam couldn't always figure everything out.

Three days later we arrived on the outskirts of Dead Horse. When we came to the outlet of the frozen Sag River we knew exactly where we were. We were close to our old campsite and we were eager to get there. Before Pam could utter a command we turned right and started loping up the river.

Come on, Douggie, speed it up, called Robert.

Yeah, shouted Matt. *Let's get moving.*

Okay, but I hope Pam doesn't get upset and start yelling at me, said Douggie.

It was as though some great power overtook us and we broke into a run, racing up the river. When we spotted the familiar buildings, we left the river, charged straight across the parking lot, climbed over a steep snowbank, slogged through several feet of deep snow, and stopped at our old campsite.

"Whew!" said Pam with a huge sigh. "That was exciting! I guess you dogs are pretty happy to be back in Dead Horse."

We were happy to be back all right but we were so tired we didn't even wait for Pam to take our harnesses off. Everyone turned themselves around in tiny, little, tight circles, packing the snow under their paws just right, and then plopped down for a snooze. We were a tangled mess of legs and lines but no one cared, not even Pam. One by one she moved along the team patiently untangling lines and gently removing harnesses. One by one she rolled each of us over on our back and rubbed everyone's tummy and one by one she thanked us for working so hard. When Pam got to me I didn't even open my eyes. I just let my body go limp and fell into a state of total bliss.

Chapter Ten

In Dead Horse Pam told us we were going to rest for a few days because the sleds needed some attention. I watched as she flipped both of them over and put new runners on their feet.

Meanwhile, Roald was passing the time digging a deep hole next to the tire of one of the big trucks and was throwing snow all over the place. All of a sudden he backed out of the hole and tossed something skyward. When it came down he snatched it out of the air and started chomping away.

Roald, there's a little foot sticking out of the corner of your mouth. What is that thing you're eating? I asked.

A vole. You know, one of those little mouse things, said Roald. When he swallowed, the tiny foot disappeared.

You're disgusting! I said.

You're just jealous because I got it and you didn't, said Roald.

The next morning, February 27, Pam loaded the sleds and we left Dead Horse for what would be the last time. Oddly, Roald didn't bark in my ear so I was hoping he had finally decided to grow up and stop bullying me. But about two hours later when we stopped for a break, he threw up and that's when I realized Roald was sick.

Yuck! Did you have to throw up right by my feet? I asked.

Roald didn't say anything. Pam walked up and checked him over.

"How are you doing, boy?" she asked.

Looking at him with his head down and his tongue hanging out, I have to admit I felt a little, teeny, tiny bit bad for him.

The next morning Roald was up to his old tricks again and he barked in my ear when we left camp. Pam scolded him, but it didn't do any good. Roald was much bigger than me and I felt completely helpless to make him stop bullying me. Later that day we picked up the last cache we had put in during our training and all that extra weight made the sleds harder to pull. The temperature climbed higher as another storm bore down on us. Maybe it was the weight, maybe it was the heat, maybe it was the fact that I couldn't get Roald to leave me alone; the only thing I knew was that I was feeling very sad. By the end of the day I had slipped into a deep funk.

After dinner Roald said, *Sojo, come on and play with Anna and me.*

I don't feel like playing, leave me alone, I said and then I curled up and went to sleep.

The next morning at breakfast Pam asked, "What's the matter, Sojo? You're working hard but you look so sad." She rubbed my neck and said, "Tell you what, today we're going to try something different and see if I can help you start feeling better."

I wanted to tell her I didn't care what she did. I wanted to tell her that I was mad at Roald, that I didn't even want to be a sled dog. But of course that would be pointless because she couldn't hear my silent words.

I had no idea what Pam had in mind but that day she made a big change. It started with our first break of the day. Every time we stopped for a break Pam always walked up to Douggie, rubbed his shoulders, and told him what a good dog he was. Then she moved along the team and gave each dog the same treatment. Dogs are very jealous and if one dog gets special treatment, other dogs don't like it and they get upset. But this day, instead of starting with Douggie, she started with me. After petting me, she went up to Douggie and then along the rest of the team. When she came to me Pam petted me again, so I got twice the attention everyone else got.

Hey, protested Roald, *how come Sojo's getting extra attention?*

Stop complaining, Roald. Can't you see your sister is feeling sad and Pam is just trying to make her feel better? said Mom.

Yeah, Roald, leave her alone, said Anna.

Day after day Pam continued to pet me twice at each break. That extra bit of attention made me feel good and gave me something to look forward to. I kept waiting for someone to get upset or complain, but no one did, and that made me feel good, too.

One day we were sledding along a beautiful beach when we came upon a bunch of trees lying on their sides. Big branches and upturned roots stuck up all over the place. We hadn't seen a tree since we left home months ago, so everyone was very excited.

What's that great smell? Hey look, there's a dead fish stuck in here! said Matt.

Everyone started drooling and sniffing around and some of us got our lines tangled up in branches.

"All right, let's go!" called Pam.

How does she expect us to move when we're all tangled up? I asked.

"Get moving!" bellowed Pam.

We couldn't get moving so everyone just kept milling about, sniffing tree roots, and ignoring Pam. In almost no time the entire team was bunched up into a tight little knot. No one else had found a fish so everyone started complaining.

I don't like being in the middle of this mess, grumbled Robert.

I simply cannot work like this, said Mom.

Me neither, agreed Lucy.

Umm, this fish is really good, said Matt.

Anna was wagging her tail and thoroughly enjoying all the commotion, but by now Pam was furious. She stormed up to us and one by one began pushing us apart and untangling our lines, but before she could get back to the sled, we had already managed to become a tangled knot all over again.

Several more times we managed to get ourselves tangled up but eventually we got tired of sniffing logs, Pam finally succeeded in getting us to stay untangled, and off we went.

Pam was in a sour mood for quite a while after that. As for me, watching all the excitement and sniffing those trees was the most fun I'd had in a long time and I think it was good for the team.

Chapter Eleven

Yahoo! We crossed the border! We're in Canada! This is our first major milestone!" shouted Pam.

What's a border? I asked. *What's Canada?*

Pam hopped off the sled and ran over to a square post that stuck out of the ground about half as tall as she was. It was painted white and had a pointy top.

"Look, all you puppy dogs. This is the official border between the United States and Canada. It even says 'Canada' on one side and 'U.S.' for United States on the other side. That way is Canada," she said pointing to her right, "and the other way is Alaska and the United States. This is a really big day!"

Canada? I thought we were in the Arctic? I asked.

We are, dear. Before we were in the Alaskan Arctic, now we're in the Canadian Arctic, said Mom.

Pam was all excited and took a bunch of pictures of herself standing by the post pointing one way with her right hand and the other way with her left hand. I could see some snow-covered mountains far away behind her and endless sea ice in front, but when I looked where she was pointing, it didn't look any different, just flat land and some low rolling hills covered in snow. Since it was a warm, sunny day, we all decided to lie down and take a nap while Pam ran around pointing and happily taking more pictures of herself.

March 11. Our first full day in Canada was a nightmare.

When we took off that morning the weather had changed completely and it was snowing so hard we couldn't see more than a few feet ahead. The tundra was now covered with soft snow and with every step we punched through the surface of the snow, making it really hard to pull the sleds. There's often much less snow on sea ice and the footing is firmer, so Pam told Douggie to take us out onto the ice. But the ice was so broken up and jumbled that it was nearly impossible to sled across.

Eventually Douggie found a narrow stretch of flat, smooth ice not too far from shore and our pace picked up. Pretty soon we saw a big, rectangular building up on the land. We could smell people and food, so we went back up on the land and stopped by what seemed to be the main door. Pam got off the sled, looked around, and told us this building was part of the DEW Line system and had something to do with the military, whatever that is.

"I'm going to see if I can find a cup of coffee and maybe a human to talk to. I'll be back in a while," she said.

Just then two huge dogs came bounding over a snowbank, barking furiously, and headed straight for Pam. She stopped in her tracks. The dogs skidded to a halt and then separated, one on either side of Pam, and began slowly circling her. The biggest one, a reddish-brown male, kept trying to close in while the other, a white female, stopped in front of Pam and stared straight into Pam's eyes. These dogs were very scary.

No one move! commanded Douggie. *These are guard dogs and they're not used to strange people or dogs. Everyone stay calm and don't bark.*

What if they attack Pam? I asked.

Then we attack, but only on my command, ordered Douggie.

In that moment a man dressed like a cook opened the door and looked out to see what was causing all the commotion. The guard dogs turned and looked at him but he just stood there watching. Then, without saying a word, he slammed the door shut and we never saw him again.

That was certainly rude, even for a human, commented my mom.

Indeed, replied Lucy.

The guard dogs swung their attention back to Pam. She had used the interruption to move a little closer to her sled. Douggie kept his eyes on the dogs and spoke just loud enough for us to hear: *All right, this has gone on long enough. I'm taking charge. Everyone swing left toward Pam just a little bit to distract the dogs toward us and away from Pam. No one is to bark or start anything without my say-so.*

When the two dogs saw us move, they charged over and started running in circles around us, barking and barking. Pam moved quickly. Once she was on the sled, the dogs knew if they tried anything we'd attack them so they backed off.

Pam shook her head in disgust. "Apparently these people aren't interested in visitors, so let's get out of here."

As we took off, the two dogs escorted us out over the tundra, always staying a fair distance behind. Later that afternoon the male dog turned around and went back home but the female kept following along. A storm had been slowly catching up to us all day so we stopped early and Pam set up camp. She fed us dinner but not the white guard dog and then crawled into her tent for the night.

Why didn't she feed that white dog? I asked.

Pam is hoping that if she gets hungry enough, she'll turn around and go back home, answered Mom.

But the next morning the white dog was still around and once again she followed us all day. By the end of the day the wind was picking up and it looked like yet another storm was coming. Late that afternoon we came to a giant, square tower with a bunch of small buildings and big machines up on top.

What is this thing? I asked.

As if she could understand me, Pam said with a sigh, "This is an oil rig. No one is on it so I guess it must be shut down. So that means no coffee and no people to talk to here, either."

The oil rig made such a good wind-block that Pam decided to set up camp right beside it. Pam didn't know the white dog's name so she started calling her Old Dog because she looked very old. Grandma Lucy didn't like other dogs around while we were eating, so Pam tied Old Dog well away from us so there wouldn't be a food fight and this time she gave her something to eat.

The storm overtook us in the night and once again we were stormbound, this time for two days. During the second day, while Pam went for a walk around the oil rig, Old Dog slipped out of her collar and came over close to us.

Get out of here, Lucy growled.

Lucy, don't growl at Old Dog, said Douggie, *she just wants some company.*

The older dogs mostly ignored Old Dog but we puppies were curious about her.

Do you live back there by that building? Who was that other dog? I asked.

Yes, I'm a polar bear guard dog with Rusty, the other dog. Our job is to bark to let the humans know when there's a polar bear around, answered Old Dog.

Wow! That must be scary! I said.

It's not so bad. Usually the bears just run off when we bark at them, said Old Dog.

How long have you been doing that? Is it fun? I asked.

A few years, said Old Dog. *At first I didn't like it because I wanted to be a sled dog and have adventures like you dogs. And Rusty used to tease me by pretending to be a polar bear and I hated that.*

Anna and Roald laughed, but I didn't. I knew how Old Dog felt and her story didn't seem funny to me at all.

Old Dog continued, *Rusty doesn't do that anymore because I finally stood up to him. That made me feel pretty good about myself so after that I quit moping around and Rusty and I became good friends.*

But weren't you sad when you realized you were never going to be a sled dog and have adventures? I asked.

At first I was but after awhile I finally figured out that it was my choice to be happy or sad. When I stopped feeling sad I started thinking of ways to have adventures.

What kind of adventures? I asked.

Sometimes in the winter groups of people come by our place so I decided to start following them and see where they were going, just like I'm doing now. One time I followed some hunters 250 miles to a town where I found some other hunters who were going the other way and I followed them back home. That's my longest adventure so far.

Wow, Old Dog! That's amazing. But weren't you afraid when you went off on an adventure? What if they didn't feed you? What if you got separated and got lost? I asked.

All of those things did happen at one time or another. But I always made it back, said Old Dog.

For a long time I didn't want to be a sled dog. I wanted to be a show dog because I'm so beautiful, I said.

Old Dog laughed. *Well, Sojo, you are a beautiful dog, that's for sure.*

Lately though I'm not so sure I want to be a show dog any-

more because I've been kind of enjoying being a sled dog. Of course I'm not anything special, I'm just an ordinary team dog, I said.

Old Dog shook her head and said, *You're no ordinary team dog, Sojo. You were selected to go on an arctic expedition and that's pretty special. You should be proud of yourself.*

But sometimes I hate being on a dog team because of my brother. Every morning when we take off he barks in my ear and it hurts. He's bigger than me and I'm kind of afraid of him.

That's hard, said Old Dog. *But, Sojo, you can't always be afraid. Somehow you've got to figure out how to stand up to him.*

Three days later we came to another one of those DEW Line places and Pam went inside to talk to the people and see about getting Old Dog back home.

When Pam came back she was laughing. "It turns out Old Dog is famous all across the Canadian Arctic and her real name is Molly. She follows anyone who passes by her home and usually shows up here at least once a year. Lucky for her, a plane will be coming through with supplies in a few days and they'll fly her back home."

Of course, I already knew about her daring ways and it was exciting to think that I had met a famous arctic adventurer.

The last time I saw Old Dog, she was following a bowl of meat scraps held by a kind looking man who led her inside the building. Her latest adventure was nearly over but I knew she would go on many more. To the older dogs in my team Old Dog was just another dog hanging around who could spin a good yarn. To Pam she was just another mouth to feed. But to me, next to Douggie, she was the most inspiring dog I have ever known. She taught me to always make the best of things and to be proud of myself, no matter what. Old Dog was my hero and I will never forget her.

Chapter Twelve

Not too long after leaving Old Dog we came to a stand of willow thickets. These stubby bushes were only about two feet tall but they grew so densely there seemed to be no way through. Nevertheless Pam told Douggie to move in. The snow was soft and punchy and nearly a foot deep. Right away the branches snagged our harnesses and the sleds got jammed against the willows. Over and over our little train got stuck and over and over Pam had to come forward and free everything up. Finally we came to a narrow channel covered in thick, flat ice.

"Everybody take a break while I figure out where we are," bellowed Pam.

She took out a big piece of paper that she called a topographic map that showed her where there were hills and rivers and coastline. After awhile she folded it up and announced, "This is the Mackenzie River Delta. It's where the Mackenzie River dumps into the sea. In the summertime trees float down this river and get swept out to sea and the ocean currents carry them west. Remember all those trees we got tangled up in back on that beach in Alaska? Well, this is where they came from."

Luckily, the delta had a bunch of these frozen channels that were connected to one another in a crazy zigzag pattern, so all we had to do was sled from one channel to the next all the way across the delta. Finally, after two-and-a-half long, hard days, we came out onto the main channel. When I looked ahead I saw a long, straight trail that stretched beyond the horizon. *Wow! This is the biggest trail I've ever seen,* I shouted. Pour Douggie looked exhausted from all the commands Pam had given him and when he led us onto that channel I could see his shoulders relax.

Pam whooped and hollered. "Yahoo!! We made it! We're on the ice road over the Mackenzie River! You can take it easy now, Douggie, because this is going to take us all the way to Tuktoyaktuk."

Zoom! A ratty old pickup truck caught up from behind and zoomed past us heading north, leaving us in a cloud of churned up snow.

This isn't a trail, Sojo. Pam said it's a road, said Anna.

Zoom! Another car zoomed past, heading south. Then another and another, each one leaving us in a cloud of snow.

Robert and Douggie were in lead, Anna and Mom were behind them, and I was right behind Anna. I began to notice a distant, low rumble. The road was covered by slick ice and we were all focused on not falling down, so I didn't pay much attention to the sound. After a few minutes it grew a little louder but still seemed a long way off.

Does anyone hear that rumbling sound? I asked. No one answered. I looked over my shoulder but I didn't see anything. Finally, we came to a long snowy patch where it was easier to keep our footing and I could concentrate on the sound.

Anna, don't you hear that? I asked.

Anna looked back over her shoulder and gasped, *Sojo, look!*

When I saw the terror in Anna's eyes, I turned my head to see what she was looking at. I couldn't believe my eyes! It was the monster from back home! The one with the big boxy face. The one with the huge flat nose. It was the monster that nearly killed me and it was chasing us!

Pam looked back at the monster and did nothing! *What's the matter with her!!? Doesn't she understand that monster is going to run us over and squash us flat? Run for your lives!* I yelled.

Douggie looked back to see what the commotion was all about and immediately took charge. *Don't worry; I'll take care of this. Everybody speed up!* he commanded.

The monster was closing in!

BEEP! BEEP! it yelled at us.

Faster! I screamed. *We have to run faster!*

BEEP! BEEP! BEEEP! yelled the monster. It was almost on top of us!

We were practically flying down the road! *Douggie, we have to get off this road now!* I screamed.

There! called Douggie. *Over on the right.*

Our heads turned as one and we saw a deep cut in the snowbank. If we could get through there and out onto the tundra we might be saved.

Just as we reached the cut Pam called, "Gee."

It's about time you said something! I yelled.

The monster was closing in. The rumble was deafening.

Now! Turn right now! ordered Douggie.

We charged through the cut and out onto the tundra.

Swoosh! The monster roared by just as the trailer sled escaped the road.

We stopped and stood staggering, trying to catch our breath as we watched the monster disappear up the road in a giant cloud of snow.

"Wow!" said Pam. "Did you see the size of the snowplow

that just passed us? That's the biggest one I've ever seen."

I don't care what you call it. I hate that thing and I never want to see it again, I cried.

Pam called, "Douggie, haw."

We left the tundra and slipped back out onto the road and continued our journey north. We never saw the monster snowplow again but soon many cars and trucks were passing us only now everyone was slowing down so we wouldn't be left in a big cloud of snow. People tooted their horns and waved at us with big smiles on their faces. I looked back at Pam and she was smiling and waving back at everyone. The people of Tuktoyaktuk were making us feel welcome and we hadn't even gotten there yet.

We got into Tuktoyaktuk early the next morning. All that day and the next Pam was very busy but we dogs just ate and napped in the sunshine. In addition to laying out caches, Pam had mailed supply bags out to schools in villages along our route and she had promised the principals she would visit the students in return for the school storing our supplies. At this school they made her a judge at their science fair and then she did a radio interview with CBC North. People were very friendly and several times small groups came to visit our camp. One even brought us a bunch of fish. The villagers were so nice, I was sad when it was finally time to go.

Our first day out of Tuktoyaktuk was miserable. The sleds were way too heavy and, to make matters worse, the land was covered by a dense fog and we could hardly see where we were going. By the end of the day, everyone was so tired we were practically falling over.

After dinner Pam looked at us and said in a not very convincing voice, "Don't worry. It'll be better tomorrow."

No dog said a word. We all just tucked our noses under our tails and went to sleep.

In the morning nobody wanted to get up. But, as all sled dogs know, we are supposed to work hard and pull when our human tells us to, so when Pam bellowed, "All right, let's go," tired as we were, we dutifully leaned into our harnesses and left camp.

Douggie had been running in lead nearly every day since the expedition began so Pam had decided to give him a rest and put my dad, Robert, in lead beside Anna. By noon we were all so bushed we could hardly see straight and Dad started messing up. When Pam called "gee," instead of turning a little to the right he would make a sharp 90-degree turn. When Pam called "haw" to get us back on course, Dad would turn 90 degrees to the left. Anna, who by now was becoming a pretty good lead dog, kept trying to make the turns the way Pam ordered but Dad kept shoving Anna all over the place.

I could see Pam and Anna were getting more and more upset. Anna kept yelling, *Dad, quit shoving me around,* and Pam was shouting commands louder and louder.

Finally, Douggie put his paw down. *Robert, Anna . . . stop. We're taking the rest of the day off.* Immediately, everyone stopped in their tracks.

I couldn't believe Douggie was doing this . . . and neither could Pam.

I glanced back at Pam and her face was now beet red. Then Douggie gave us our orders. *Everyone lie down. No matter what Pam says, no matter how loudly she yells, don't get up.*

With that we all curled up and stuck our noses under our tails.

Pam got off the sled and charged along the team waving her arms and shouting. I have always thought of Pam as a lady and so, to preserve her reputation, I feel it is best that I not reveal what she said to us on that blustery afternoon. When she finally stopped shouting and looked up and down the team, nobody moved a muscle. But every eye was on Pam, waiting to see what she was going to do next.

Amazingly her face softened as she realized her mistake.

"Okay, this isn't working. There's too much weight on the sled," she said. "We're taking the rest of the day off AND we're taking tomorrow off, too."

True to her word, we stayed in camp the next day. Everything was perfect. The temperature was mild, there was no wind, the sun broke through the fog, and after Pam fed us breakfast, she turned us all loose! The minute she unleashed me, I squinted my eyes, stretched my long legs, and ran. I ran farther and faster than anyone. And then we played. Oh, how we played. We chased each other in circles, we jumped over one another, and wrestled for hours.

We were so happy we didn't even feel tired anymore. We ate huge chunks of dog-food pizza for lunch and then we ate even more. By early afternoon we had finally worn ourselves out so everyone lay down and took a nap. We must have been quite a sight, eight sled dogs scattered around camp all stretched out and sound asleep in the afternoon sunshine. It was a day filled with bliss and one of the happiest memories of my entire career as a sled dog.

But what I remember most was what happened after dinner.

As soon as Pam said good night to us and crawled into her tent, Douggie called a team meeting. We all waited silently, wondering what he was going say.

Soon we will be sledding through an area that has a lot of polar bears, he began. *The males will be far out on the sea ice hunting seals so it's unlikely we'll meet any of them. Most of the mother bears will be in their dens with their cubs, but it's very close to the time when they start bringing their cubs out. Those dens are just snow caves in hillsides close to the ocean and, since we usually travel along the edge of the ocean, there is a chance we may see some bears. A mother with cubs can be a very dangerous animal, so we're going to have to keep a close eye out for the next couple of weeks.*

Have you ever seen a polar bear? I asked.

Yes. Once a polar bear came right into our camp, said Douggie. *She tore Pam's tent to shreds and caused a lot of damage.*

Did Pam kill the bear? asked Roald, his eyes bugging out.

No. Pam said the bear was young and acting like a curious dog and it wouldn't be right to shoot her. Now that took some courage, said Douggie.

Anna's eyes were wide in amazement. *So, what happened to the bear?* she asked.

After awhile that bear walked away and we never saw it again.

Is that really true? I asked, feeling a little doubtful.

Yes, it's true, said Douggie.

Douggie glanced at my mom and she nodded.

Tell them, Douglas, said Mom. *Tell them about Pam.*

Douggie looked down, took a deep breath, and sighed. Finally, he shook his head and said, *Ever since that encounter, Pam has been afraid of bears.*

No, that's not true! shouted Robert.

Pam's not afraid of anything! I said.

You take that back! cried Anna.

Douggie looked around at us and said, *I know it's hard to believe, but I'm afraid it is true. So we must always remember, if we see a bear it's our responsibility to stay away from it. Pam depends on us to keep her safe.*

What should we do if we see a bear? I asked.

Mostly likely we'll see it when it's still a ways off, so just follow my lead and I'll keep us away from it and there shouldn't be any trouble, ordered Douggie.

We all sat silently for a long time thinking about Pam and polar bears. If Pam was afraid of them, they must be very dangerous.

I hope we never see even one bear on this trip, I said.

Douggie looked at me and said, *I hope so too, Sojo, but this is the Arctic and we know they're out there somewhere.*

Looking out into the darkness that surrounded us, I felt a little scared.

Chapter Thirteen

For the next week we traveled east. Each day the sleds got lighter as we ate our way through the dog food. And each day was pretty much the same—breakfast, travel, lunch, nap, travel, dinner, sleep.

On April 1 we were enjoying a calm and uneventful day of sledding. For several hours we moved through a wide, flat river valley. The temperature stayed a pleasant two degrees below zero, a gentle breeze kept us cool, and by late in the afternoon, the fog that had been shrouding us all day finally burned off, revealing a clear, blue sky.

We emerged from the river valley onto a flat, wide, frozen beach with just a dusting of snow. To our right were short bluffs with snow-filled gullies and to the left rose jagged chunks of piled-up sea ice. The beach before us looked like a superhighway and I could see Douggie's shoulders relax.

We were moving along at a nice pace when Pam suddenly stopped us, walked to the front of the team, and made the most astonishing announcement: "Anna, you've been working so hard lately I think you deserve a break, so I'm taking you out of lead and putting you in swing for a while. Robert, you get to run in lead beside Douggie. There's nothing but a straight beach in front of us so you should do fine. Just pay attention when I give commands."

I looked at Roald and whispered, *I can't believe Pam is doing this again. Dad's terrible at following commands.*

I know, whispered Roald, shaking his head. *Maybe he won't mess up this time.*

Pam climbed back on the sled and bellowed, "All right, let's go."

Robert and Douggie led us down the beach and everything was just fine for, oh, maybe five minutes when we sledded around a big curve.

Look at that! cried Robert, looking off to his right.

I looked right and there up in a gully stood a mother polar bear nursing her cub. Yikes! Those bears were maybe just a hundred yards away!

Robert swung a hard right.

"Robert! Haw!" Pam commanded.

Robert paid no attention and pulled even harder.

Robert! What are you doing? Douggie shouted in alarm.

"Haw! Douggie! Haw!" shouted Pam.

Douggie kept trying to lead us back on course to get us away from the bears. Everyone was getting more and more excited as we swung closer toward the bears.

Dad! What are you doing? I shouted. *Go left! Go left! You're going to get us killed!!*

"Douglas! Haaaw!" Pam yelled in desperation.

Douggie was completely overpowered by the team. Before we knew it, we were racing across the beach heading straight for the polar bears!

I could hear the sled brake grating on the beach as Pam pushed down hard with her foot, trying to stop us. But there was only an inch of snow on the beach and nothing for the brake to dig into.

Within seconds we reached the bottom of the gully. As we tore uphill toward the bears, the brake suddenly dug into some deep, wind-packed snow and we jerked to a halt. But it was too late! Douggie and Robert were only about three feet from the bears! In a panic everyone began barking wildly and lunging at the bears. Everything was completely out of control.

Pam was screaming, "Haw! Douglas! Haw!" Now even Douggie wasn't listening!

The bear backed up the hill, keeping her little cub behind her.

We kept barking and lunging. I was terrified! *What's the matter with these bears? Why don't they run off like Old Dog said they would?* I watched in horror as the bear ran straight at Douggie and rammed her head into the right side of his face. The force sent Douggie sprawling downhill, dragging the rest of us with him.

The bear turned and ran back to her cub. We chased after her but we couldn't get to her because the brake was still stuck in the snow.

Then she started to drool. You would have to be there to believe how much drool can come out of an agitated polar bear's mouth. It was like four water faucets going off at the same time! Gross! Then the bear began wagging her head and clawing at the snow.

Douggie shouted, *Everybody quiet down.* But Robert and Roald kept barking.

You guys, shut up! I shouted.

The bear jutted her heard forward and made a loud, coarse "Hiiiiisssssssssss!"

That sound scared Pam. She reached into her sled bag, pulled out her shotgun, and aimed it at the bear!

Suddenly, everything got quiet. No more hissing, no more barking . . . just silence. For the first time the bear noticed Pam. With its coal black eyes fixed on her, the bear took one step toward Pam. She stepped away from the sled and took one step toward the bear.

Everyone stay quiet and don't move, ordered Douggie. *This is very serious.*

Bravely, with her hand stretched out like a policeman stopping traffic, Pam said to the bear, "It's okay. It's okay. We're going now."

Something happened in that moment. It was like the bear somehow understood that Pam didn't want to hurt her or her cub. I watched in amazement as the bear turned and started walking toward her den opening just seventy feet away. The little cub stared at me for a moment and then chased after its mother.

Pam put her shotgun away and came up along our right side. We were a tangled mess but she quickly got the lines straightened out and jumped on the sled. No sooner had we started to move than the sled runners hit something under the snow and made a loud thud. The sled jerked to a halt.

By now the bear had reached her den opening but when she heard the sound she stopped and looked back at us.

Robert and Roald began barking and the excitement started all over again. Just as Pam freed up the front of the sled, the entire team suddenly swung hard to the right and charged the bear. Pam grabbed the gangline and was instantly swept right off her feet. One of her legs got caught in the line and the next thing I knew we were rocketing back up the slope, dragging Pam helplessly toward the bear.

Thud! Again the sled runners struck something under the snow and everything jerked to a halt. Pam untangled her leg and jumped up, frantically searching for the bear. Thankfully, it had already disappeared inside its den.

But the little cub was still racing across the snow after its mother. It had had its first lesson on how to be a big tough polar bear and, when it reached the den opening, the little cub stopped, turned to look at us, and made a tiny "Hisss!" And then it jumped into the den.

Pam grabbed Douggie's harness and swung us back around. She jumped on the sled and we took off as fast as we could run. We all wanted as much distance between us and those bears as possible. We didn't stop running for three hours.

When Pam finally stopped us to set up camp she didn't say a word but her eyes still looked fearful and I could see she was badly shaken by all that had happened. When she checked out Douggie's head she found a quarter-sized hole in his right cheek where the bear had struck him.

"Poor, Douggie," said Pam. "You certainly didn't deserve this. Here, swallow this pill so you won't get infected." Then she gave Douggie a big hug.

Later, after we had eaten and Pam had gone inside her tent for the night, we held a team meeting.

Douggie took charge and said, *What happened today was inexcusable.*

Everyone sat in silence with our heads down.

Douggie turned his swollen face toward Robert and said, *Everything started with you, Robert, when you didn't follow commands.*

I thought those bears were dogs, said Robert. *I just wanted to go visiting.*

Visiting? Visiting!? That's your excuse? You almost got us killed, yelled Douggie.

I didn't mean to cause trouble, whined Robert.

Silence! Douggie ordered.

I had never heard Douggie speak like this before and his anger startled us.

The fact is you were given a command and you didn't follow it! I will not run in lead with you again until you learn how to be responsible.

Robert was so humiliated he turned his face away from the team and dropped to his belly.

But Douggie wasn't finished.

As for the rest of you, our job is to take care of Pam and keep her away from bears. Today we failed. We failed! You all know commands and you should have helped me when I needed you. But instead you followed Robert. You know what you did was wrong and I am ashamed of every one of you. From now on, pay attention and do your duty as sled dogs!

Douggie's scolding stung. But everything he said was true. For the next three days, as we headed for the village of Paulatuk, we were all pretty quiet as we pondered our failure.

When we arrived, Pam went to the health clinic and spoke with the nurse about Douggie's wound. When she came back to camp she told us, "The nurse said since Douggie is already getting antibiotics there isn't anything else to do for him and that he should be okay." That was a big relief but we still felt bad about what had happened to Douggie.

By now we were all working very well together as a team. Anna was working as an assistant lead dog almost full-time now and I had learned so much about being a sled dog and felt so good about myself that I almost never thought about being a show dog anymore. But there remained one big problem. Roald. Every morning he was still barking in my ear when we took off and I was sick of it.

One day as Pam finished tying down the sled loads, he barked really loud and it hurt more than usual.

Please stop doing that, Roald, I said.

Roald just looked at me, smiled a big doggie smile, and barked again.

Sojo, remember what Old Dog told you? You've got to figure out how to stand up to him, said Anna.

I asked him to stop, but he won't.

Sojo, if you don't stand up to him, he's never going to stop bullying you, said Anna. *You're such a fraidy-cat.*

Don't call me that anymore! I cried.

Well, that's what you are, said Anna.

I am not! I shouted.

Fraidy-cat, fraidy-cat, teased Anna.

Stop it! I cried.

That night in camp I felt so sad I didn't even finish my dinner.

Chapter Fourteen

A few days later we were resting on a beach in the sunshine while Pam explored an old, abandoned boat we had come across. I started thinking about Old Dog and how she had stood up to Rusty, the dog that had bullied her, but I didn't believe I could ever be as brave as Old Dog. When Pam came back and got us up to leave, Roald looked at me with a devilish smile and barked in my ear. Without even thinking, I whipped my head around and barked right in his face.

Whoa, little sister. Feeling a little touchy, are we? said Roald, taunting me.

I looked straight ahead as we took off. Something in me changed in that moment. I remembered the words of Old Dog—*You can't always be afraid. You've got to figure out how to stand up to him.* In camp I didn't snuggle up with anyone and lay awake most of the night thinking and planning. Maybe I wasn't as smart as Anna, maybe I was just a team dog, but I wasn't going to be a fraidy-cat anymore. I made up my mind . . . in the morning I would show them.

I ate breakfast without saying a word to anyone. Pam packed the sleds and put our harnesses on and as usual I was next to Roald. Just as Pam reached for the snowhook, Roald turned his head and blasted me right in my ear.

I spun around and threw myself at him.

"**Bark! Bark!**" I screamed.

Roald backed up. His eyes bugged out and his mouth gaped open.

"**Bark! Bark! Bark!**" I screamed again.

Roald turned his head and tried to get away, but I kept crowding him. I took a deep breath and shoved my mouth right up against his ear.

"**Bark! Bark! Bark! Bark!**"

Roald lunged to the right, to the left, to the right. But it was no use. He couldn't get away.

"**Bark! Bark! Bark! Bark! Bark!**"

Roald was desperate. He threw himself over on his back and lay motionless with his tongue hanging out of the side of his mouth. I straddled him with my front legs and glared down at him.

Don't you move so much as a muscle, I said through clenched teeth.

Roald's ear must have been ringing because he made the mistake of shaking his head.

"**BARK!!!**"

You make one more move, you bark at me one more time, and I'll make worm bait out of you! I snarled.

The whole time, Pam and the rest of the team had stood watching in stunned silence.

Roald lay perfectly still in a show of total submission. I raised my head in triumph and looked out over the tundra as though he didn't even exist.

But I was not finished. I turned my head and looked

straight at Anna and said, *As for you, get one thing straight—
I'm no fraidy-cat.*

Anna stared at me with wide eyes. She glanced down at
Roald and then back at me. Anna nodded her head and in a
quiet voice said, *I can see that, Sojo.*

I tried my best to look calm but inside I was cheering,
Woohoo, that felt good!

Without looking at Roald, I casually moved over and let
him get up. From that day forward, no one ever called me a
fraidy-cat and Roald never barked in my ear again.

Chapter Fifteen

The Arctic seemed to be playing with us. Sometimes the weather was clear then we'd have several days of dense fog and then it would clear up again. But every day it got a little bit warmer, threatening to melt the snow and ice out from under us. The one bright spot was that things were better between Roald and me now and we three puppies were back to playing together every evening after dinner.

Working in the heat made us feel tired and we were all getting a little weary from traveling on so long a journey. On May 8 the temperature climbed so high that the unthinkable happened. It rained. Not just a little sprinkle but a heavy downpour that went on for hours, soaking everyone and everything. As if that wasn't bad enough, a powerful storm followed, dropping the temperature below freezing and leaving the Arctic covered in a thick layer of slick ice. It was almost impossible to stand up, let alone pull a sled, so Pam set up camp. Inside her tent she turned on her camp stove full blast and began the slow tedious process of drying her soaked clothing.

The next day the temperature rose above freezing again and a few inches of fluffy snow fell, making the ice even more slippery and causing us to make almost no progress. That evening we camped at a place called Half Way Point near some low hills covered with giant boulders.

As Pam was setting up her tent she started telling us what was up ahead. "You see that hill over there?" she said pointing to a steep, ice-covered slope. "If we can even get over that thing tomorrow and slide down the other side without getting injured, we have to sled 200 miles across the sea ice of Queen Maud Gulf to get to land again."

Pam reached into the sled bag and pulled out the thermometer. "The temperature is 34°F. People keep telling me it will get cold again and there'll be plenty of ice to travel on. . . . I sure hope they're right," she said shaking her head.

What no one knew right then was that something worse than rain and melting ice was about to happen. Something so terrible it would make all our other worries seem unimportant.

The next morning, we could hear a clicking noise coming from behind two huge boulders that were right behind our camp.

What's that clicking sound? I asked.

That's the sound of caribou walking. Their ankles click with each step. There must be a small herd of them behind those big boulders, explained Mom.

When the sleds were loaded, Pam took Douggie by the collar and slipped his harness on. Just as she was going to clip the tug line to his harness, two caribou emerged from behind one of the boulders. They startled Douggie and he leaped forward, jerking his harness out of Pam's hand.

The caribou were as surprised to see Douggie as he was to see them.

"Douggie, come," called Pam.

Douggie looked at Pam, then back at the caribou. The caribou stood motionless.

"Douggie! Come here!" Pam called sharply.

Douggie didn't even look back. He charged the caribou. The caribou turned and fled across the tundra with Douggie in hot pursuit.

I couldn't believe what I was seeing. Douggie, the dog who was always so dependable, our leader, my hero, had just run off after a bunch of caribou.

Pam harnessed us all in a flash. She disconnected the trailer sled and we took off after Douggie. Anna was in lead by herself and I was right behind her running as fast as my legs would go. Douggie and the caribou swung to the right in a big, wide arc and headed back toward the boulders. Anna swung the team right to try and head them off, but we were no match. The caribou ran up a steep hillside with Douggie close on their heels and quickly disappeared among the boulders.

Anna stopped the team and said, *The sled can't go between all those boulders. I can't take us any farther.*

"Douggie! Douggie, come back," Pam yelled.

How could he go off and leave us like that? I asked.

No one answered. Everyone just stood staring silently at the empty hillside in disbelief at what had just happened.

For three days we searched for Douggie. Then we sledded to a nearby town where Pam posted a $500 reward for anyone who found Douggie and brought him to us. Pam said it was nearly every penny she had but she was willing to give it all if we could get Douggie back. While we dogs waited on the beach beside the town, Pam and two men drove snowmobiles back to where Douggie had disappeared. They drove all over, searching, but the land was empty.

Finally, after six days passed with no sign of Douggie, Pam stood beside us on the beach and said what no one wanted to hear. "Douggie is gone. We have to accept that we are never going to see him again and it's time to leave this place. It's going to be hard for everyone but Douggie gave his life for this expedition and we owe it to him to do our best to finish."

But we don't have a lead dog. How can we go on? I asked.

Pam looked at Anna and said, "Anna, you're lead dog now. I know it's a lot to ask but I think you can do this. The rest of you can help Anna by doing your jobs as best you can."

Just then a man with his wife and daughter drove up on a snowmobile and the man said, "We saw your dog."

Pam looked at him in astonishment. "You did? Where?" she asked.

"Back by Half Way Point," said the man.

Douggie was alive! Pam leaped on the sled, called a grateful "thank you" over her shoulder, and we took off. In all my life I have never seen a team of dogs run so far and so fast as we did that day. We made an all-time record of seventy-two miles before stopping for a few hours of sleep! But when we arrived at Half Way Point the next morning, there was no sign of Douggie.

I thought Douggie was supposed to be here, I said.

That's what we all thought, said Mom.

What do we do now?

He has to be here somewhere, said Anna. *We're going to search until we find him.*

For three days we searched but found nothing. Then one day a group of snowmobilers came by and one of them told Pam that Douggie had found his way back to the village we had visited before the rain.

Pam gasped, "But that would mean he traveled 135 miles alone over a trail washed away by that rainstorm."

The man smiled and said, "Pretty amazing dog you've got there. Anyway, the people in the village have him and they know where you are camped. They'll bring him here tomorrow morning."

We all felt happy but we didn't celebrate. There had been too many disappointments. By noon the next day when no one had showed up, Pam got us ready and we took off heading toward the village where Douggie was supposed to be. Almost as soon as we left camp I spotted a snowmobile coming toward us. Pam saw it too and she told us to stop. Behind the snowmobile was a trailer sled. On that sled was a box and in the box was Douggie. Or *was* it Douggie?

When we all met, Pam got off her sled and walked over to the box where a black dog sat staring at nothing. The man who had been driving the snowmobile helped Pam lift the dog out of the box and place him on the snow. Pam checked the dog over and then gently led him by the collar to where we were waiting.

The dog was black like Douggie but this dog was skinny and his coat looked scraggly. He didn't raise his head to look at us, he just stood there looking beaten down and weak. But mostly it was the dog's eyes that made us wonder who he was. There seemed to be no intelligence, no confidence, they just looked empty.

For a little while no one moved. We were uncertain what we should do but then, ever so slowly, we eased forward and gathered around the dog, carefully sniffing him. His scent was all we needed because our noses never lie. Yes! This sad, pathetic looking dog was indeed Douggie!

Douggie? I asked softly. *Don't you know us, Douggie?*

Too much had happened to Douggie and he was in a state of shock. For what seemed like a long time we all stood there silently surrounding Douggie, our leader, our teammate, our friend. Finally, ever so slowly, he raised his head and looked at me as though waking from a dream.

Sojo? he asked in a weak voice.

Yes, Douggie, it's me, I said.

I'm here, too, said Anna.

We're all here, Douggie, I said. *We've been searching and searching for you. We've been so worried. To get you back is the best thing that could ever happen.*

Pam set up camp and fed Douggie several small meals over the next couple of days. We tried to get him to tell us what had happened while he was lost but he said he was too tired for storytelling. So we left him alone to rest and regain some of his strength. As it turned out, we would never know what happened to Douggie during his terrible ordeal because for the rest of his life he refused to talk about it.

Chapter Sixteen

It was getting warmer by the day, so we needed to get going.

Pam checked Douggie over and said, "Douggie, I can see you're not strong enough to work so you just walk along and do your best to keep up. Anna will lead the team until you get your strength back."

Douggie looked at us and bravely said, *I'll get strong again, you'll see.*

Douggie was still our teammate and we all loved and respected him. But from that day forward Anna would remain number one lead dog.

We made it over the icy hill and out onto Queen Maud Gulf where the ice seemed thick and strong and the first day we made good progress. But soon the temperatures got so high that the top few inches of ice turned into a nasty mess of ice water and coarse slush.

Dragging sleds through slush is backbreaking work and our feet hurt from walking in the slush. It rained almost all day every day and every day our mileage dropped. There was never a good place to camp anymore so Pam would search until she found a slab of ice that rose out of the slush and we would climb up and rest there for a while.

Everywhere there were seals lying on the ice next to their breathing holes digesting the fish they had caught. Since seals often have eight or ten breathing holes and can hold their breath for up to twenty minutes at a time, we were never any threat to them. Nevertheless, when they saw us coming they would dive through their hole into the sea where they would swim to another hole farther away.

It continued to rain almost all day every day and soon cracks began to appear in the ice. At first they were no problem and we could easily step over them but as the ice continued to melt, the cracks got wider and wider. Many times Pam would get off the sled and jump over the cracks while we dogs made a run for it, leaping from one piece of floating ice to the next, pulling the sleds and all our supplies behind us. This was very dangerous because the water was almost 200 feet deep.

If the crack was so wide that Pam didn't think we could make it, we would turn and sled along the crack until we found a narrow enough place where we could jump over. One day we came to one of those really wide cracks and for some reason Pam didn't give a command to turn.

Anna, I called, *look to your right. There's a place over there where the crack is narrower. I think we can make it across there.*

Sure enough, when Anna led us over to that place, we were able to easily jump across.

It's really hard to know how thick or strong sea ice is when it's melting because ice melts from the bottom and the top. One day we came to a wide crack with a big piece of ice floating in it. We had often used pieces like that as a sort of bridge to scurry across. It looked pretty wobbly to me but before I could say anything, Pam told Anna to move forward.

The instant Douggie and Anna stepped on that chunk of ice it broke apart and they fell through into the icy water! It happened so fast Robert and I couldn't stop and we fell in, too! We were all thrashing around in a panic. Anna and Douggie swam to the far side of the crack and managed to climb out onto the ice. That stretched the sled lines tight, pulling Roald, Matt, Lucy, and Mom to the edge of the crack. Pam screamed "Whoa! Whoa!" and pulled back on the lines, trying desperately to keep them from being dragged in. Everyone was freaking out.

I shouted, *Douggie, Anna! You've got to come back this way! You're going to pull the rest of the team in.* They both stood there looking at the freezing water and I could see they were too frightened to jump back in.

Just then Pam grabbed the lines and yanked. Douggie and, Anna went into the water with a huge splash. I suddenly felt myself rising out of the water as Pam grabbed my harness and, with one mighty heave, lifted me up onto the ice beside her. I shook and shook trying to get the water out of my fur but I was still freezing cold. One by one, Pam pulled Robert, Douggie, and Anna out of the water. I couldn't believe it when Pam grabbed our lines, got us all sorted out, and made us go back to work.

Can't we stop and rest? I begged.

No, Sojo, said Mom. *Your fur will dry out faster and you'll warm up quicker if you keep moving.*

It was a sweltering 42°F so we didn't have to sled very far before our fur was completely dried out. Douggie was staggering with exhaustion and we were all still shaken by our near tragedy, so Pam finally stopped us on the next big slab of ice so we could lie down and rest.

The problem with all the zigzagging along cracks and leaping from one chunk of ice to the next was that we weren't making much forward progress and we were getting further and further behind schedule. During the break Pam looked around at the melting sea ice and told us something we didn't want to hear. "We've been out on this ice for a week and we should have reached the other side of Queen Maud Gulf by now, but we still have over twenty-five miles to go. The way we're moving, it will probably take us at least three more days to reach shore. Even if we make it, we don't have enough dog food to last that long so everyone is going on half rations. Only Douggie gets full meals."

Everyone groaned. Our morale was already low and this just seemed to be too much for the team. When Pam gave the command to head out, no one moved.

Matt, who loved to eat more than anything else but hardly ever complained, got very upset. *We're wet from constantly walking in water, we're exhausted, and now we have to go hungry?*

How are we supposed to work if we don't get enough to eat? asked Roald.

I'm not pulling those sleds another inch, declared Lucy.

Me neither, said Robert.

Everybody settle down! shouted Anna. *We'll die out here if we quit now. At least we're going to get half rations. Has anyone noticed that rotten odor we've been smelling for the past couple of days? That's Pam's food gone bad. She has almost nothing to eat. We have to work together as a team so we can get ourselves out of this mess. We've come a long way together and I know we can finish this trip.*

I was so proud of my sister. She was taking charge and giving us encouragement like a good lead dog should do.

Anna's right, I said. *We have to stick together and keep trying.*

With our heads and tails down, we slowly moved off the slab and into the slushy water. Two days later it was Douggie's tenth birthday but we were too exhausted to celebrate.

The ice was now so thin and broken that every day at

least one of us fell into the water but we always managed to get out one way or another. Pam never rode the sled anymore; she just walked along hanging on to the sled handle. One day when she stepped on what looked like a pile of slush, she plunged into the icy water. She managed to get herself out and kept going just like the rest of us. Incredible though it may seem, falling into freezing water wasn't a big deal anymore.

By June 6 so much ice had melted we were standing in water up to our bellies and the sleds were floating when Pam called, "Whoa." There was an odd smell in the air. It was the hard, sour smell of rock!

I raised my head and looked across the water. *Look, everyone! Land!* I shouted. *We're almost there!*

At first everyone got all excited but after only a few minutes of pulling, we came to the edge of the ice. There was no way to cross the open water and get to the land.

"Anna, haw," said Pam in a quiet voice.

We turned left and started moving along the edge of the ice looking for a way over to the land. In the distance was a small gravel peninsula that stuck out nearly to the ice we were sledding on and I was certain we would be standing on dry, solid land very soon.

But we were so worn-out none of us was paying much attention to what we were doing.

Suddenly I heard a loud splash!

Anna had fallen into a seal hole and disappeared beneath the water!

Everyone stared at the hole in disbelief.

Suddenly Anna shot to the surface coughing and gasping for air. The water in the hole was spinning like a whirlpool, threatening to pull her back down. Anna dug her front claws into the ice and tried to pull herself out, but the ice was too thin.

Crack! The ice broke under her weight. She fell backwards into the water. She tried again and again but the ice kept breaking.

Pam rushed forward and grabbed Anna by her collar. **Crack!** When she lifted her out of the water the ice broke under Pam's feet. Anna and Pam started to sink. Pam threw herself sideways and scrambled back to stronger ice but she lost her grip on Anna's collar and Anna fell back in the water.

Pam ran back to the sled and yelled, "Haw! Douggie!"

Douggie turned to the left and pulled. His tug line was connected to Anna's line so if he could pull hard enough he could save Anna.

"Haw! Douggie! Haw!" Pam shouted.

Douggie pulled and pulled as hard as he could. But he wasn't strong enough and he couldn't pull Anna out.

Pam was desperate. She screamed again, "Douglas! Haw!!!"

Anna looked at me and I could see she was terrified. She cried out, *Sojo! Help me!*

Anna is drowning! I shouted. *We have to save her. Come on, everyone. PULL!*

Anna's head was sinking beneath the surface. She couldn't last much longer in the freezing water.

Anna, when we pull, you have to help us, I yelled. *Pull, everyone, pull!*

Anna dug her toenails in and lifted herself with all her might. The team pulled with everything we had. We kept pulling and pulling. Anna kept lifting and lifting. Inch by inch Anna was coming out of the water. **Crack!** The ice broke and Anna slipped back under the water.

Pull! Pull! I screamed. Finally, with one last mighty heave, we dragged Anna from the water.

She lay on the ice limp and unmoving.

I poked Anna gently with my nose. *Anna? . . . Are you okay?* I asked. Were we too late? Was Anna dead?

Finally, Anna took a breath and then another and another. Slowly she struggled to her feet and shook herself off. *I thought I was a goner but I'm okay now,* said Anna with a weak smile.

Pam ran up and used her mittens to soak some of the water off Anna's coat. Her voice shook with emotion as she tried to hold back her tears, "Oh, Anna. That was a pretty close call, girl. But you're going to be okay."

Oh, it wasn't so bad, said Anna. She looked at me and said, *Thanks, Sojo. You saved my life.* Then she shook one more time and went right back to work with the rest of us like nothing even happened. I have to admit, my sister is pretty tough.

Very soon we reached the little peninsula and saw that it came almost right up to the ice. With a single leap, each of us made it to land and we were finally safe. After we rested for a while, Douggie came up to me and said, *Sojo, the way you took over and got everyone working together back there, that was very impressive. You acted like a lead dog and I'm proud of you.*

Thanks, Douggie, I said with a big doggie smile.

I looked over at Anna lying on a patch of gravel and said, *But it wasn't just me, Douggie; everyone did their part. But I'm not a leader, I'm still just a team dog.*

Douggie put his face down next to mine, looked me straight in the eye, and said, *Sojo, we all know you didn't want to be a sled dog. But you still worked hard and did your job every day and you seldom complained. Everyone on this team has a lot of respect for you. You used to be so afraid that you would never be a good sled dog, but, Sojo, you've got what it takes. No matter what position you work in, you have become a **first-class** sled dog.*

That was the proudest moment of my entire life.

The land we had made it to was King William Island. It was sometime in early June but we had lost track of dates because Pam had been too exhausted to keep up her daily announcements of dates and temperatures. We spent the next five and a half months living in the small Inuit village of Gjoa Haven where Pam stayed with a kind and generous family and we dogs stayed just outside of town in a place called Dog Town where all the village dogs lived. Over the summer everyone rested and Douggie regained his health. In the fall when the sea ice was strong enough to travel on, we trained for a few weeks and then one day Pam made one of her announcements.

"It's December 5, it's -34F°, and it's time to go," she said. And just like that, we left King William Island to finish our journey.

On January 9 we arrived safely at our destination of Repulse Bay, Canada. It had taken us eleven months to cross the Arctic but we had finally succeeded in completing our 2,500-mile journey. It was the longest solo dogsled journey by a woman in recorded history and the first time an American had dogsledded solo across arctic America.

As for me, watching my teammates happily wagging their tails, surrounded by a small group of people who had come out to congratulate Pam, I realized how much confidence I had gained on our journey and that I was proud to be a sled dog.

PART THREE

Forever Young

Chapter Seventeen

Everyone was ready to go home, but there was just one problem—Pam had no money left. We were lucky though and we were given free passage on a plane south to Churchill, then we got to ride on a train to Winnipeg, Manitoba, where Pam was given the use of a big truck so she could drive us across Canada and home to Alaska.

On January 19 Pam opened the back of the truck and I turned my head to look out, figuring this was just another rest stop along the highway. Instead I saw the most beautiful sight in the whole world—Pam's cabin. We had left here 14½ months ago and now we were finally home!

Group howl! I shouted.

We were so happy, we threw our heads back and howled what I think must be the longest and loudest howl of any dog team in history.

The rest of the winter was spent

mostly relaxing in our dog lot and only going for the occasional short run around our neighborhood. In the winters to come, some of us would go on other journeys but none as long or exciting as the one we had just completed. The next eight years brought a lot of changes and the older dogs, Robert, Douggie, Matt, Lucy, and finally my mom passed away.

One day Anna looked around the dog lot and said, *It's lonely around here with so many dogs gone.*

Yeah, I know. But, at least we still have each other, I replied.

It would have been easy to get depressed, but I remembered Old Dog telling me that we always have choices. I missed my teammates very much and sometimes I felt sad, but life goes on and eventually I always chose to feel happy again.

There were a lot of good things to feel happy about, like when Pam built us a huge pen so we could run around and play like when we were puppies and we were never chained up again. Every morning Pam would open the gate to our pen to let us out and we would go with her on long walks. When blueberries were in season we would head down the road and wade into the patch where we dogs would pucker our lips and suck the berries off the bushes while Pam tried to pick a few before we got them all.

But I have to admit we were not always perfect little angels. One day while we were walking along the road, we saw something kind of brown-colored sitting on a big rock right beside the road and we took off after it. Bad idea.

Pam called, "Roald, Anna, Sojo! Get back here!"

But we were so excited to see what it was, we didn't pay any attention to her. Roald ran over and barked at it. Bad idea.

When I got closer and saw what it was, I yelled, *Yikes! It's a porcupine!*

The poor little thing was so frightened it leaped off the rock and ran into the forest. Roald tore after it. Another bad idea.

Roald! What are you doing? Leave that thing alone! I yelled after him.

A few minutes later Roald came charging out of the forest with the porcupine in his mouth! *Very* bad idea. He opened his mouth and shook his head back and forth until finally the terrified porcupine dropped out. It escaped back into the forest but this time Roald was smart enough not to run after it.

By now Pam had finally caught up to us and she stood there with Anna and me gaping at poor Roald's face. He had quills sticking up through the top of his snout, one stuck out right beside his eye, and several were sticking through his lips. Blood was dripping from the end of his nose where a big cluster of quills were stuck.

When Pam pried his mouth open, we all gasped. *Oh, Roald!* I said, *the entire roof of your mouth is covered in quills and they're stuck every which way all over your tongue!*

Roald was hysterical and crying pitifully. He kept shaking his head and sticking his tongue out in a hopeless attempt to get rid of the quills. Needless to say, Roald made a fast trip to see Angela, the veterinarian, who gave him medicine to calm him down while she pulled out every quill. When Pam brought Roald home, his nose had a very different shape. It looked kind of like the big, round, slightly torn ball we played with.

Chapter Eighteen

We had lots more little adventures close to home but, of course, we were also getting older and one day Anna passed away and then Roald. I was very sad but I still had Pam. We spent a lot of time together and we grew much closer as friends. I remember one day when I was sixteen years old, after filling up on blueberries and taking a long walk in the cool of the evening, I was unusually tired. After Pam went to bed, I crawled up on the couch and went to sleep. I dreamed I was someplace really foggy and I felt as though I were floating away on a cloud.

Then the fog cleared away and you'll never guess who I saw!

Anna! Is that you!

Yes, Sojo! It's me! said Anna with a big smile. *I told everyone you would be coming along soon. Look over there, do you see them?*

I could hardly believe my eyes! Running across a big, wide field straight toward us were Robert, Douggie, Matt, Lucy, my mom, and Roald! Everybody gathered around and we sniffed noses and wagged tails and it was wonderful to smell everyone again.

Wow! I can't believe we're all together again! I shouted.

We've all been waiting for you, said Mom.

This place is great, said Roald. *I can bark all I want and it doesn't hurt anybody's ears.*

And I don't get into trouble for not following the rules because there aren't any rules, said Robert.

Lucy nodded and said, *I don't have to steal steaks anymore because they're free for the taking up here.*

Sojo, said Douggie, *you're going to love this place because everyone is free to run anywhere they want for as long as they want. In fact, we're going for a run right now. Would you like to come along?*

Thanks, but I'll catch up later, I said. I watched all the dogs run off across a beautiful field that seemed to stretch forever. Only Anna lingered beside me, patiently waiting.

When I turned my head and looked back into the fog, Anna asked, *You're thinking about Pam, aren't you, Sojo?*

I nodded.

Don't worry, said Anna with a kind smile. *This is heaven and Pam will be along soon enough. In the meantime, let me show you something really special. Over here we have a dogsled and every once in a while we all get together, step into our harnesses, and drag it around like in the old days.*

Wow! That sounds like fun, I said.

It is, said Anna. *Well, I'm going for a run, Sojo. Why don't you look around and make yourself at home.*

As I walked around, I could see why everyone was so happy. There were doghouses filled with lots of straw and couches for dogs who preferred those. Everywhere there were bowls overflowing with liver treats, hamburgers, and steaks and there were piles of big meaty bones to chew on. Blueberry patches and raspberry patches loaded with ripe berries stretched over the horizon. Every dog had a human to walk with, and give them belly rubs, throw balls, make sure their water bowl was full of fresh cool water, *and* those humans could hear everything a dog said.

Off in the distance I noticed a dog team running toward me being led by a young white dog. As they drew closer I could hardly believe my eyes. *Old Dog! Is that really you?* I shouted.

Old Dog pulled up and stopped her team in front of me. *Yes, it's me, Sojo. I've been up here for a while now having one sled dog adventure after another. I've got to run but we'll see each other again.*

Watching Old Dog leading her team away brought back so many wonderful memories. I drew in a big breath and sighed as an old familiar feeling swept over me. I felt like a young dog again and I could not resist the urge. I squinted my eyes, stretched my long beautiful legs, and I ran as fast and as hard as I could. I felt as though I could run forever.

Then suddenly it was a little foggy again and something was touching my shoulder. I could hear Pam's voice gently calling, "Sojo, wake up, girl. It's time to go for our morning walk."

I opened my eyes, rolled off the couch, and headed for the door. My legs felt stronger than they had in a long time and I felt happy, even sort of blissful.

Pam smiled as she opened the door and said, "You must have been running in your sleep, Sojo, because your legs were twitching like crazy."

As we walked down the driveway together, I looked up at Pam and said, *I dreamed I was running in heaven. It's the most amazing place. Everything is perfect and all the humans can hear dogs talking and. . . .*

Of course she couldn't hear me, but I know now that one day she will.

Author's Note

Most books about sled dogs focus on the lead dog or some dog that unexpectedly saves the day. Seldom does anyone write about an ordinary team dog like my dog Sojo, who spent her life working hard and quietly doing her job. We've all seen dogs approach one another, do a quick sniff, and then engage in some activity—growling, playing, circling, or walking away—and we humans are often left wondering what just happened. Long ago I came to realize that there is a secret world that only dogs know, so I thought it would be fun and challenging to write a story from a dog's perspective. Because this is a memoir, Sojo tells about many events that happened in her life instead of focusing on one particular event. Her story helps us understand not only the secret world of dogs but how Sojo became the dog she turned out to be.

Sojo was named after Sojourner Truth, the famous abolitionist and equal rights advocate. The last living member of my dog team that traveled alone across the Arctic with me, Sojo was born January 19, 1992, and passed away September 16, 2008. I still miss her very much.

Our adventures are told in five books: *Alone across the Arctic, Big-Enough Anna, Douggie, Ordinary Dogs,* and *Sojo* (which, like *Big-Enough Anna*, is illustrated by my friend Bill Farnsworth). I hope you enjoy them!

Glossary

CACHE: A place where provisions are placed for later use.

COMMANDS: The words used by dog drivers to tell their lead dogs what to do.

DEW LINE (Distant Early Warning Line): A series of radar stations built across Alaska and Canada during the 1950s as part of a military defense system. Most are now abandoned as new technologies have made them obsolete.

GANGLINE: A series of ropes running from the front of a dogsled. The dogs are attached to the gangline by short lines that are clipped onto their harnesses. Dogs usually run in pairs, one dog on each side of the gangline.

FOUR-WHEELER: A four-wheeled, motorized vehicle that the dog driver uses to train sled dogs. The driver sits on top and the dogs are attached to the front of the four-wheeler by a gangline.

LEAD: An opening of water in sea, river, or lake ice.

LEAD DOG: A dog that runs in the front position in a dog team and follows commands given by the dog driver.

SEA ICE: Ice that forms when ocean water freezes.

SLED BAG: A heavy cloth bag that is placed on the sled and cinched down tightly with rope to contain gear and keep out snow.

SLED BRAKE: A three-pronged metal claw that is attached to the floor of the sled and used to stop or slow the sled when the driver presses down with one foot. A spring holds the brake up when not in use.

SNOWHOOK: A heavy, two-pronged, iron hook attached to the sled with a rope. It is used to anchor the sled by jamming it into the snow.

SWING DOG: A dog that runs directly behind the lead dog and helps the lead dog swing the team.

TEAM DOG: A dog that runs in the middle of the team.

TOW LINE: The part of the gangline that runs through the middle of the team and has a series of shorter tug lines attached.

TUG LINE: A short line coming off of the tow line that is attached to the dog's harness.

TUNDRA: Treeless plains of the arctic region, with low-lying vegetation on top of cold, often frozen soil.

WHEEL DOG: A dog that runs directly in front of the sled or four-wheeler.

Discussion Questions

1. Sojo was born in a litter with a brother and a sister. Describe the three dogs. In what ways are they the same? In what ways are they different? Give examples from the story to support your ideas. Which of the three dogs has a personality most like yours, and why? (4.RL.3, 4.W.9a)

2. Early in the book, Sojo thinks she'd rather be a show dog than a sled dog. How are these two paths different for a dog, and what qualities are needed for each? (4.RL.1, 4. RL.4)

3. Describe the steps taken to train the puppies to be sled dogs. What was the purpose of each step, and how do you know based on the text? (4.RL.1, 4.RI.3)

4. How would you describe Pam's relationship with the neighbor, Dave? Why do you think the author included him in the story? What pieces are you told directly by the author, and what do you have to *infer*? (4.RL.1, 4.RL.3)

5. Write a descriptive paragraph about the puppies' first experience in an arctic blizzard. Do not use the author's words for your description. Instead, put yourself in the puppies' position, and help the reader feel what is was like that night. (4.RL.3, 4.W.3, 4.SL.2)

6. What is dog-food pizza? Describe the steps Pam takes to make it, and explain why it is used on the journey. (4.RL.1, 4.RI.3, 4.W.9b)

7. What was the temperature on the day the sled team set out over the tundra? How does that compare to the average temperature where you live? How does the weather (including the temperature) affect the dogsled team over the course of the book? (4.RL.1, 4.RI.3, 4.W.9b)

8. Who is Old Dog, and what lessons did Sojo learn from her? (4.RL.1, 4.RL.3, 4.W.9a)

9. What did Roald do to tease or bully Sojo? How did Sojo eventually get him to stop? (4.RL.1, 4.RL.3, 4.W.9a)

10. The dogsled team has lots of tough challenges on their trip across the tundra. Describe one problem the team faced, and explain how they solved it. (4.RL.1, 4.RI.5)

11. How would *Sojo: Memoirs of a Reluctant Sled Dog* have been different if it had been written from Pam's perspective? Why do you think the author chose to tell the story from the position of a dog rather than a human? (4.RL.6)

12. At the beginning of the book, the narrator says, "All the stories in this book are true. Well, okay, I admit I took a few liberties here and there, but mostly they're true." Which parts of the story do you think were true, and which parts were embellished by the writer, and why? (4.RI.1)

13. Compare *Sojo: Memoirs of a Reluctant Sled Dog* to another book you've read featuring an animal. How were the

books the same? How were they different? (4.RL.9, 4. RL.10)

14. What is one major theme of this story? What main idea do you think the author wants you to take away? Support your answers with examples from the book. (4.RL.2)

15. Why was this sled team's journey considered historically important? Give details from the book and/or outside research to support your response. (4.RL.1, 4.RI.10)

CPSIA information can be obtained at www.ICGtesting.com
Printed in the USA
BVOW06*0949220916

462975BV00006B/16/P

9 781943 328550